HELLO,

CRUEL HEART

An original tale by

MAUREEN JOHNSON

AUTUMN
PUBLISHING

AUTUMN
PUBLISHING

Published in 2021
First published in the UK by Autumn Publishing
An imprint of Igloo Books Ltd
Cottage Farm, NN6 0BJ, UK
Owned by Bonnier Books
Sveavägen 56, Stockholm, Sweden
www.igloobooks.com

Autumn is an imprint of Bonnier Books UK

Cover designed by Soyoung Kim

0421 001
2 4 6 8 10 9 7 5 3 1
ISBN 978-1-80108-036-1

Printed and manufactured in the UK

For Gig. Thanks for all the music. It's been great.

1

ALL THINGS FOR ALL PEOPLE, EVERYWHERE

"ALL RIGHT, you," a voice said.

Sixteen-year-old Estella turned and found herself facing one of the Harrods security guards, a red-faced man with a heavy moustache.

"I beg your pardon?" she said, aghast. "Please take your hand off me."

She said it loud enough that several people turned. A tourist raised a camera, so the man pulled on Estella's bag strap to manoeuvre her several feet away, out of view.

The guard had the right idea: Harrods, the great London department store, was not the place where one wanted to make a scene. Especially not in the thick of summer, when the store was swarming with tourists from all over the world.

"The bag," he said. "Open it."

"I will not," she said shortly. "I'll speak to your supervisor about this!"

"Open that bag."

Estella sighed.

Things, admittedly, had gone awry.

Estella had been following along dutifully as a woman in a pink sheath, her ginger hair piled high and teased into a bubble dome, made her way from counter to counter, purchasing cheese, overpriced biscuits, candied fruit and pickled nuts. They'd advanced all the way to the seafood counter, where the woman was grilling the seafood man about the freshness of his fish.

Harrods' motto was, after all, 'Omnia Omnibus Ubique', or 'All things for all people, everywhere' (though its motto should have been "All things for all *rich* people, everywhere").

The 'all' was quite literal: if one could dream it – and pay for it – Harrods would sell it to you.

Satin and furs? Of course.

Shoes, coats and hats? Naturally.

A toy car? A real car? An airplane? A yacht? All available.

A coffin? A tiara? A lion? A gold bar? Harrods could accommodate.

But nowhere did the store take its motto more seriously than amid its large food halls, seemingly miles of elegantly tiled floors that supported the very best and most varied comestibles England – and the world – had to offer. There was the proud stink of the cheese counter, the swoosh of knives being sharpened by the butcher and more than a rainbow's worth of colours in the sweets department.

And there was Estella, in her green school skirt and blazer. Her copper hair was long and straight with fringe, in a fashionable cut modelled after the capital's most famous redhead: Jane Asher, Paul McCartney's glamorous girlfriend. Estella was enjoying the cool of the seafood counter, laden as it was with ice packed around the glassy-eyed fish on the warm Friday afternoon. She took her relief where she could get it.

"How fresh are your oysters?" the pink sheath-clad woman asked the man behind the counter.

"Extremely, madam," the man replied. "Fresh this morning."

The woman stared at the lumpy oyster shells as if she desired them to speak for themselves.

"Are you *sure*?"

"Quite sure, madam."

The woman, engaged in her interrogation of the oysters, handbag hanging limply from the crook of her elbow, paid no mind to Estella, unremarkable in her school uniform. The handbag had a simple clasp top, the kind one could snap open in a second. Those handbags were an absolute gift to the pickpockets and petty thieves of the world. The man behind the seafood counter also paid Estella no mind, because Estella's hair was as bright a shade of orange as the woman's. Who else could Estella be but this wealthy customer's daughter?

Such a simple trick, and it worked every time.

Estella slid closer, making a great show of interest in a large lobster that rested miserably on the ice. Just a few inches more...

Then the tourists arrived.

"This way! This way!" A voice boomed from the entrance to

the hall. "This way, ladies and gentlemen! Watch yourselves, come through, come through, right this way."

A man holding a small flag reading SWINGING LONDON TOURS led a group of about fifty people into the hall. The visitors marvelled at the scene unfolding around them. They oohed and aahed at the endless counters of food. They raised their cameras and snapped photos.

The woman at the seafood counter turned sharply, and her handbag went with her. It was between her body and the glass now, just out of Estella's reach.

"Oh dear god," the woman said, looking at the group. "Those ghastly people. Why do they let them in here?"

The question was rhetorical, and the man behind the counter did not reply.

The tourists massed in the hall, taking up all the free space and air. They were dressed in formless travelling clothes – grim dresses and even grimmer trousers and shirts. Estella made a note of this because she simply couldn't help it. She always analysed every cut and every stitch of every outfit that passed her. Her mind was a whirling calculation of fashion.

Estella made clothes. Very good clothes. Possibly the best clothes in all of London – not that London knew it yet.

Some of the tourists approached the seafood counter.

"Would you look at that!" one of the men said with a broad American accent. "All that fish!" The group murmured in rapturous agreement, equal measures shocked and delighted by the fact that there was seafood at a seafood stand. They would never get over it.

"I'll just get some smoked oysters in tins, then," the ginger-haired woman snipped before striding off towards the tinned foods. Estella sighed and followed, growing bored. Why was it that the gingers, who provided Estella the best cover, were always the most particular and picky? Surely it wasn't a *ginger* thing.

As she made her way after the woman, one of the tourists from the group waved at her. "Miss, would you mind taking a picture with my wife?" he said.

Estella should have said no. She was busy. She'd been tailing her mark for over twenty minutes, and the goal was close at hand. But the man looked so enchanted by her. There it was: the antidote to her ennui – the opportunity to perform. To be darling. Plan be dashed. Estella liked to live in the now.

"Oh!" Estella said. "Oh. Yes! Of *course!*"

"Look at your tie!" the wife exclaimed, practically

clapping her hands in excitement as Estella positioned herself next to her. "Girls wear ties here?"

"For school," Estella replied politely.

"Do you guys want a picture with the British girl?" the wife shouted eagerly to her friends. "Millie! Jake! Just look at her! She's wearing a *tie*!"

Estella stayed still for several minutes, losing her ginger-haired cover but gaining an entire cohort of loud, brassy American fans. She went from one to the next, smiling, posing – the perfect English teenager.

Then, suddenly, she saw a head in the distance, scanning, looking for her. Red face, sporting a big moustache, that she knew all too well.

Red Face's eyes locked on to hers. It was time to go.

"Oh," Estella said, "my mum. I've lost her. I have to go find her."

"Of course." The group waved her off. "Have a nice day!"

Estella worked her way through the crowd. At first, she was polite, saying "excuse me" in a moderate tone as she pressed towards the door. But then she became more insistent, and then she stopped asking altogether and simply pushed her way through. She was so close – the great heavy doors just steps away. She knocked herself through them, taking a deep filling breath of the muggy London air as she made it outside.

Then she felt something pulling her from behind. Someone had the strap of her bag. She couldn't move.

"Open that bag."

Estella's expression changed from one of righteous anger to something a bit more flinty.

"You're out of your jurisdiction," she said, her voice no longer plummy and posh. Now it was pure rough London.

"The pavement under the awning is still Harrods property," Red Face replied. "And I can call the police if that's what you want. There are loads nearby. Here..."

He used his free hand to fish a whistle from his pocket and raise it to his lips.

"Fine," Estella said, flapping open the bag. "Here. Have a look."

Red Face reached into the bag, examining the contents. There was a French book and a pencil case.

"Turn out your pockets."

"I have rights, you know," Estella said, but she emptied her pockets just the same. A small crumpled piece of paper fell out. Red Face bent over and picked it up.

"Now what's this?" he said, opening it.

The paper read *I love coppers.*

Estella smiled widely at the guard's ever-reddening visage.

"I do love the police," she said, her rich, plummy inflection returning.

"What did you do with it?" he shouted. "I saw you!"

"Saw me what? Dirty old man, watching young girls like me."

"I saw you take that tourist's wallet," he fumed. "I know I did."

"The heat must be affecting you," she said, fluttering her eyelashes.

"Get out of here," he said, reddening even further. "And if I see you back in here again, I'll…"

"Turn into a giant raspberry? Do a dance? Grow wings and a beak? Do tell. What will you do?"

Red Face started to raise the whistle to his lips once more, so Estella broke free and backed up, making her exit.

"Goodbye, darling," she said, blowing him a kiss. "I'll never forget our time together."

When Estella had gone, a puzzled tourist approached the guard.

"Do you do that to everyone when they leave the store?" he asked. "Is that an English thing?"

2

THE TERRIBLE PARTY

ESTELLA SLIPPED up Brompton Road, mixing into the crowd of students all dressed as she was, in emerald-green uniforms, green-and-gold-striped ties and flat boater hats. Most of them had removed their blazers in the heat, and she did the same. Estella felt coursing through her the light, loose joy she experienced each time she got away – the closer the call, the bigger the buzz.

A double-decker bus bearing an advert for the new Beatles album, *Sgt. Pepper's Lonely Hearts Club Band*, passed

by. The Beatles had taken to wearing fabulous new clothes –
Edwardian military uniforms in lime green, fuchsia, electric
blue and peachy red. Something was happening now, this
summer of 1967. London had become the coolest place
on earth. The press called it Swinging London. No more
stodgy grey clothes. No more sombre expressions or polite
restraint. No more rationing, no more quiet dignity. It was
like *The Wizard of Oz*, when everything went from the black
and white of Kansas to the sudden, saturated colours of a
strange new land. London had the fashion, the music, the
scene; the whole world wanted to see the show. Hence the
large groups of tourists.

There was a rich fullness of life that could not be denied.
It was everywhere – in the colours of the clothes and the
buses and the trees in the park, in the smell of the earth
turning over after the rain, in the feeling of the crowd of
students Estella had fallen in with. She wasn't one of them,
really, but she had slipped into their raucous, jostling current,
their spirits buoyed by the school year's approaching end.
She felt almost like she understood their personal jokes,
like they were letting her listen in. On that kind of day, you
couldn't turn anyone away. The youth of London was one
great, moving force, and everything was wonderful.

The students headed for Hyde Park, as they did each day after school. They went to relax by the Serpentine, the little stream that ran through the park, where people could hire boats and generally lounge around on a fine afternoon like that one. Estella dropped onto the grass nearby, not with them, but close enough to feel like she might be part of their scene.

A few minutes later, two boys her age, also in school uniforms, came along and dropped down beside her. One was tall and lanky, with a sharply jutting chin and a shock of brown curly hair. The other, stouter and with a ruddy complexion, looked incredibly pleased with himself.

"Thought you had it that time," said Jasper, the taller one. "Did you really have to start posing for photos? What are you, a pop star?"

"I didn't want to disappoint the tourists," she replied.

"Risky. He was right on you."

"I knew where he was," Estella said. "I had plenty of time to get away."

Horace took her satchel. While it had appeared empty to the Harrods security guard, Horace reached inside a hidden lining and produced several items. He counted. "Six wallets," he said, "a watch, some of these traveller's cheques... no good, them... but at least fifty quid."

"Oh, and this..." Estella reached into the waistband of her skirt and produced the slender leather wallet she had removed from the tourist's pocket right by the door as she was rushing out. She tossed it to Horace, who eagerly went through it.

"There's another thirty quid in here!" he said.

Jasper stretched out his long body on the grass and smiled up at the sun.

"I love tourist season," he said. "Going to be a good one this year. Swinging London forever!"

"This keeps up," Horace added, "maybe we can get a car! Imagine having a car!"

"What would you do with a car?" Jasper asked. "You can't drive."

"I'd learn. I'd drive around."

"Probably into a post."

"I wouldn't," Horace said, injured. "I could learn."

"Please tell me you brought me something to eat," Estella said.

Horace produced a paper bag that contained a sandwich wrapped in greaseproof paper.

"Canned meat and mustard," he said, handing her the sandwich. "Extra mustard, all full of pepper."

She unwrapped it quickly. She was starving. Estella liked strongly flavoured things, lots of mustard, so much it almost made her sneeze. She liked pepper most of all. She put it on everything, loads and loads of it in amounts that would make other people cough and gag.

Jasper and Horace went on about the things they might do with all the takes they were sure to haul in that summer, all the things they would get. A proper telly. New shoes. Estella ate her sandwich and felt the sun on her skin. It had been a good day for them. Takings like this would keep them well. Tourist season was always good, but now that London was the most popular place on earth, things would be even better.

The students around them were having a good time, laughing, talking, gently pushing each other. One of them had a portable radio that was playing a song the announcer had introduced as "Everybody's Sun" by a group called the Electric Teacup. By the squeals that erupted from some of the uniformed girls, Estella gathered this was a popular band, or at least a popular song. The lyrics were a bit cloying – something about tea and the sun belonging to everyone. But there was something about the tune that caught her imagination. There was a happy piano jangle, but underneath was the echo of an organ – a deeper, more shadowy version of the same melody. The bass line snaked through, hypnotic. The song might have been squeaky clean on the surface, but there was something else going on, something dark and playful, like a shared joke intended only for those who opted to hear it.

"I love this song," one of the girls said. "They're better than the Stones."

"You're mad," another protested.

"I'm not. He's got a better voice than Mick Jagger."

The group debated the merits of various bands while Estella watched them subtly. What would they do that evening? Some would go home to their nice houses. Some would go away for the weekend. She supposed a lot of them would go out at night to one of London's many clubs to listen to music and dance. They seemed so happy all together. A pair of them were side by side on the grass, the boy's head dipping towards the girl's as they whispered intently to each other. What did she care about that romantic couple whose young love was surely doomed? Or, for that matter, the students in general? After all, a long time ago it had become painfully clear that school – and the kids who went there – was not going to work out for Estella.

In fact, that was how it had all started.

It was not Estella's fault. Truly. Mostly everything that had gone awry in her life to date could be pinned on her hair – her *real* hair – black on one side, white on the other. It made her stand out, and not in the way she meant to stand out.

Estella was a visionary. A genius, if she was being honest. She should have been noticed for being the most gifted, creative person in school. Instead, she was the scholarship charity case with skunk hair.

It didn't matter how many times her mum, Catherine, had told her she had as much right to be at her posh school as anyone else. They came for her as soon as she arrived – the bullies.

To repeat, it was not Estella's fault.

If they spat at her – and they did – there would be repercussions.

If they framed her for a mean prank on a teacher – and they did – she would be forced to take action.

If they chucked her into the rubbish bin – and they did – she would need to respond. Even if being in said rubbish bin did result in Estella's happening upon Buddy, her dog and most trusted companion.

Estella had taken care of those bullies. She had plotted her revenge carefully, even though Catherine begged her not to. And the revenge had been sweet. It had also marked the end of her school career. Fortunately, Estella's mum had pulled her out of the school before they could expel her – about five seconds before they expelled her, but it still counted.

The truth of the matter was that Catherine had seen it coming, even if Estella had not. Catherine, who had taught Estella how to sew at a young age, had at first encouraged her to follow the patterns and cut along the lines, but it soon became apparent that Estella could follow no pattern but her own. Her designs were better, more inventive. Catherine knew that Estella needed a bigger stage, a chance to make it in the world. So when Estella's short and scandal-ridden school career came to an abrupt end, Catherine figured she would give in to the fates and use it as an opportunity to greet the inevitable. She would give Estella's talent a chance to flourish as it deserved.

Catherine had packed their possessions into their shabby little car, and the two – plus Buddy – had set off for London. Estella had felt a momentary pang of sadness as she and her mum left their little house for the last time, but that faded quickly as they pulled onto the motorway and she saw the first sign pointing the way towards London.

London. The capital. The place where everything happened. The future. Something had bubbled up inside Estella then – an excitement so pure that it felt like it was buoying her up, carrying her out of the car and lifting her all the way up to the clouds. She and her mum shared a smile, both feeling the magic of that moment – the misting rain a magical silver, a theatrical fog that would soon part to reveal the marvellous thing beyond. Everything was ahead of them.

If only they had driven straight to London, things would have been fine.

"I need to make a stop," Catherine had said, "on our way into the city. Ask a friend for a little help to get us on our feet."

"What friend?" Estella asked.

Her mum did not give a direct answer. Instead, she pulled the car through a set of massive gates. Estella saw a strange symbol on them – a family crest with a three-headed Dalmatian, like the hound that guarded the gates of hell, but in the form of the black-and-white spotted dog.

It was weird.

Estella soon forgave the oddness of the crest when she saw the house the drive belonged to. It was grand on a scale Estella had not been aware of. She would never forget the sight of the old mansion against the night sky. The outline of the building looked like teeth. Every window was lit from within with an almost otherworldly glow. She heard music flowing from inside, filling the air around the manor. Other cars pulled up along with theirs, but they were expensive. And out of them stepped the most extraordinary people. (Well, possibly the most ordinary people in the most extraordinary clothes. Estella was awed into silence all the same.)

Everyone was dressed as if they were in the court of Louis XVI – the women in tall powdered wigs and incredible massive dresses of chiffon and fur. And so many colours! That shocking pink with the trails of sky blue. Violet with gold. A delicate leaf green with a buttery yellow.

"Stay in the car," her mum had instructed.

That was the only thing she had to do – stay in the car. So simple. And Estella wanted to be good; she really did.

But the moth must go to the flame. Nature demanded it.

Estella had to get a better look at those dresses. Every part of her screamed and ached to see them up close, or at least a little closer. So she stepped out of the car, Buddy in tow.

Getting into the house was no problem. Estella trailed some servers bringing in supplies and slipped through a massive kitchen, lost in the flurry of activity. Twelve-year-olds, after all, could easily make themselves invisible in the world of adults. They barely had to try.

From the kitchen, she was able to get into the main part of the house – if it could be called a house. Most houses did not have grand ballrooms of swirling marble with sweeping staircases. Most houses could not stage fashion shows with large catwalks, where models strutted up and down, showing off the latest season's creations. As Estella watched the proceedings, rapt and open mouthed, a woman who was dressed more beautifully than anyone else in the room, and who appeared to be more important than any of the other attendees, was lowered from the ceiling on a swing. "Let them eat cake!" she cried. She landed gently on the staircase, where a trio of Dalmatians awaited her.

There was, indeed, a massive cake, and all the attendees

cheered. The scene was so utterly overwhelming that Estella temporarily forgot her mum, her order to stay put, and everything else in her life.

And it was in that moment that it all went wrong.

It wasn't Buddy's fault, either. How could he resist chasing a dress trimmed in whole squirrel furs? Calls of nature such as that must be obeyed.

He leapt up onto the runway, and Estella had to chase him. She tried to get him to heel, to no avail. It was, if she was being honest, very funny to see the models go flying and the staff running after her. And who could resist knocking over such a massive cake?

It would have been one of the highlights of her short life, except that in the next moments those ferocious Dalmatians were coming after her and Buddy. The pair ran from the house into the night, where they took refuge in the shrubs.

All right. Maybe she should have stayed in the car.

Then Estella saw something that made no sense: her mum and the regal-looking woman from the swing were outside together, having some sort of heated discussion. They were right on the edge of a cliff, lightning flashing overhead. The Dalmatians appeared again, tearing across the lawn. But they did not head for Buddy and Estella. This time, they turned towards Estella's mum and the woman.

The last image Estella had in her head of her mum was of the Dalmatians heading straight for her, and Catherine's graceful, lithe form tumbling over the side of the cliff.

Something inside Estella told her to run. She raced across the grounds with Buddy right beside her. There was a vehicle coming; she saw the headlights. Estella and Buddy managed to jump onto the back of the lorry.

Estella's next recollection was of the sounds of traffic. She peered under the canvas and saw she was in London. The lorry was passing by Regent's Park, a landmark she'd pointed out to her mum in the guidebook she'd been paging through in the car, so when the lorry stopped at a red signal, she and Buddy jumped off. She walked to a fountain, which splashed gently. It was so soothing, and she was still so exhausted, that she stretched out next to it and returned to sleep.

When she woke again, there was a small dog with an eye patch staring down into her face. Then a tall boy started walking towards Estella. She snapped her eyes closed and pretended she was still asleep. She could sense the boy was standing by her.

"Morning," he said.

Estella did not move.

"So," said another voice, "what's she?"

"Watching us," said the tall boy. "But pretending to be asleep."

"Undercover copper?"

"Too scared-looking to be a cop."

That was too much for Estella.

"I'm not scared," she said, still squeezing her eyes closed.

"Also," the boy added, "looks to be only around twelve, so possibly too young."

That was *really* too much to take. No one told Estella she was scared, and no one made light of the fact that she wasn't yet fully grown. She sprang to her feet, facing the two boys down. She was pleased to see the alarm in their faces at her sudden movement.

"Stay back!" she said.

Buddy growled in her defence. The strange little one-eyed dog took up position in front of the boys.

"I'll just take her out," the second boy said.

He stepped towards her. Estella immediately kicked

him in the stomach. The first boy squared off with her, his hands raised.

"Look, luv," he said with a thick London accent. "The cops come by at eight a.m. every day, like clockwork. You should come with us."

The second boy, still gripping his stomach, looked at his friend in disbelief.

"No way! Go back to your family, little girl."

"She has no family," the first boy said.

She has no family. The words rang inside Estella's head. He was right. Her mum was gone, disappeared off the side of that cliff. That was why she was there.

She was alone – alone in the world. She had no one except Buddy, who pressed his furry body against her shins, sensing her pain.

"How do you know?" the second boy asked.

"I recognise the look."

His perceptive kindness was too much. She would not start crying. She would *not*. Because if she did, she would never stop.

Just then, the police turned up.

"Five to eight," the tall boy said. "That's unfair." He

turned to Estella. "You need to run. We all need to run. Now!"

That was the first time Estella ever ran from the police, though it was certainly not the last. The two boys were Jasper and Horace, and they had all been together ever since that moment. The trio had soon grown inseparable. Jasper and Horace became more than Estella's friends – they were her family, filling the Mum-shaped hole in Estella's life as best they could. They were all she needed. With them, she was content and happy. She didn't miss anyone from her past life – except for her mum – and she definitely didn't need anyone else.

Definitely.

"If we take in enough, we could even buy a motorbike..." Horace was saying.

Estella blinked once, then again, having got lost in staring at the pair on the grass. They weren't kissing. They were talking. It was intense. In some ways, it appeared more intimate than kissing. What were they saying? What did you say to someone when you were that close to their face? What was that important thing, that secret, that—

"Oi!"

A crumpled bit of paper hit the back of Estella's head.

"You with us?" Jasper said. "Want to head home?"

Estella popped the last bit of sandwich into her mouth, then stood up. She brushed the dirt off her skirt and, with her head bent down, sneaked one final, covert look at the couple. They didn't notice. A monster could have emerged from the Serpentine and they probably wouldn't have seen it.

"Come on!" Jasper said.

Estella shook off the sudden feeling of disquiet that had overtaken her. She was not going to let herself get bogged down staring at other people and thinking about what they might have, or who they might have, or the choices she'd made in life that had set her apart from them.

London was swinging that summer, and Estella was going to swing right along with it.

3

RED OR YELLOW

THERE WERE many worlds within London.

The starch-white buildings that formed the crescents around Piccadilly Circus, a bright, loud intersection of screaming adverts for soap and makeup and shows.

The palaces and parks full of ducks and swans and people sitting in the sun.

The golden-red brick terraced houses of Kensington.

The twisty-turny, gritty area of Soho, where the environment suddenly shifted to dark nooks and corners and wonderful, terrible things – and just as abruptly switched back upon exit to an entirely typical museum or a street of expensive shops.

And then there were places like the one Estella, Jasper and Horace lived in, which they lovingly referred to as the Lair: places that had experienced a rain of bombs in the war more than twenty years before, places that had never been repaired. The building they lived in was really half a building; a bomb had come and simply taken away one entire side, leaving the other half with the strange imprint of the missing structure. There was a patchwork of paint and wallpaper that indicated where rooms had once been: a pink square, a patch of rose-flocked wallpaper, a China blue. There were traces of stairs, funny zigzags, linking the patches together. Very few people wanted to live in half a building, so this one had fallen vacant and been left to decay. It became the property of squatters, vagrants and general ne'er-do-wells. Eventually that included Jasper and Horace, and then, finally, Estella with them.

On that hot summer afternoon, the ne'er-do-wells in question were studying the day's haul, which was spread out on their rickety table. They each took some money for themselves; the remainder went into a jar. The watches and other goods were separated out. Those would be sold to a few friendly vendors they knew.

Then it was time to relax. Jasper went to their record player.

"Whatcha like?" he asked. "Rolling Stones? Beatles?"

The selection of music in the Lair was not large. Mostly they listened to the radio. But they did have three albums.

"Beatles," Estella said, her tone brooking no argument as she crossed the room to her sewing table.

"We should get that new one they've got out. What's it called? Captain Beetroot or something?"

"Sergeant Pepper."

"That's the one. We should get that. We have a bit of extra dosh."

Jasper and Horace's one-eyed Chihuahua, Wink, was asleep in a basket of fabric beside Estella's sewing machine.

"Shift it," she said to Wink. He wasn't supposed to go in there, but every time they went out, he sneaked in for a nap. Wink hopped out without protest and wandered to his bed, which was just another pile of fabric and old clothes.

Estella's part of the Lair was the most crowded. Her bedroom wasn't much aside from a lumpy bed and a bedside table. But her work area consisted of her prized sewing machine, endless piles of cloth and several mannequins. Shops got rid of them more often than one might have thought. No one wanted to see a mannequin whose head was permanently backwards because of an ill-thought-out attempt to have it looking to the side, or whose arm slid out of the sleeve and landed on the floor. They tossed those, and people like Estella dragged them out of the rubbish. Her mannequins were not entirely stable and were reinforced by rope and hanger wire. It wasn't how Mary Quant worked, probably, but it still got the job done. (Of course, getting them home was another matter. That sort of thing had to be done under the cover of darkness, as it was quite suspect to drag what appeared to be a lifeless body into an abandoned building.)

Estella caught a glimpse of herself in her mirror before she sat down. "I need to do my hair again," she mused.

She went into the bathroom and retrieved a box of red hair dye from under the sink. Estella had to use it every few weeks; otherwise her natural black-and-white colour would start peeping through. No one could ever see her real hair, because once seen, it could not be forgotten. And to be unforgettable was generally a very bad thing for someone in her line of work.

Going copper had been the product of a moment's deliberation. When Estella had first arrived in the Lair, Horace had proffered two containers of dye they happened to have around, one red and one yellow. She took the red one. It had taken some time and trouble to get the dye just right: the white side of her head came up bright like a bus, and the black side a muddy, confused maroon. But Estella worked at it, as she worked at everything, and soon it was a consistent, deeply hued copper – not altogether unattractive on her, she had to admit.

Estella squeezed the tube of foul-smelling dye into her hair, rubbing the chemicals in from root to tip as she scrutinised her reflection in the bathroom mirror.

"So what are we hitting tomorrow?" Jasper asked, climbing with his guitar in tow into the hammock strung up across the beams. "British Museum? Always good on a weekend. Nice and crowded."

"Boring, though," Horace said, his face already buried in a *Beano* comic. "Just a bunch of rocks and things."

"Whatcha think, Stel?" Jasper said.

"The museum always works," she said, wrapping her sticky hair in a rubber cap. "But the weather is so good. We could try Regent's Park. Or St James's Park, then do the crowds in front of the palace for the Horse Guard."

"Oh, I do like a palace crowd," Jasper said. "Horace?"

"Yeah, that one. Park and palace. At least we can get an ice cream."

Hair securely wrapped up, Estella returned to her sewing table and finished some new disguises with hidden linings. After working on those, she moved on to a new dress she was making – not a disguise, but one of her own personal designs, for the simple sake of creating something.

It was a patchwork – not a quilt, but a mosaic. She had got the idea from the outer wall of the building, actually, noticing one day that from a distance, the side of the building reminded her of a garden. She realised that she had many extremely tiny pieces of fabric in a variety of colours and patterns (Estella kept every remnant, no matter how large or small – a holdover from when she'd been a child and used the scraps from her seamstress mum's floor to concoct her creations), and began to lay them out on paper on the floor, then worked out the design of a dress that looked like a tangle of flowers in full bloom. From a distance the picture would be clear, but the closer one got to the dress, the more the separate prints and patterns revealed themselves.

It was detailed, complicated work, and Estella had been at it for weeks between jobs. She was so close to being done. There was just one small section that wasn't quite right. It was making her frustrated.

Fortunately for the dress, Estella wasn't one to be deterred by frustration.

Hours later, Estella stretched her arms over her head, her back cracking in a satisfying way. The afternoon and evening had slipped away into night-time. Jasper and Horace were already snoring in their beds. She'd made some progress, but not enough. It was never enough for Estella until it was absolutely perfect. She rubbed her eyes and pushed back from her sewing machine.

"Time to eat," she said to Buddy.

Buddy, relieved that he could finally leave his post by the sewing machine, followed her as she shuffled to their little kitchen. She filled Buddy's dish with dog food. There was some cold spag bol sitting on their hot plate.

Estella took the pot, sprinkled loads of pepper on the gluey noodles and lumpy red sauce, and ate her supper cold. It was impossible to know whether Buddy or Estella had the more palatable meal.

From there, she went into the bathroom and filled their old tub with lukewarm rusty-tinted water for a bath. Nightfall had brought no relief from the day's soaring temperatures, and it was stifling in the Lair. Not even splashing in the tepid water stopped the sweat from rolling down her back. She scrubbed herself clean as best she could, changed into a loose nightgown, and headed for bed.

It never got completely dark in the Lair. There was a large circular window that had no covering. Estella stared out at the night sky and the moon that hung over London. She wasn't tired. Her thoughts wandered, eventually returning to the couple entwined with each other on the grass. What might that be like, to be part of that couple, one half of a whole? How could they be like that, so unreservedly giving of themselves, willing to share their innermost wants and fears with another person?

Because they were normal, Estella thought. Because they went to school and had homes. They didn't live in lairs with boys they had met on the street. They didn't pick pockets for a living. They would go on to do normal things. Estella despised the thought of normal – but in this case...

... perhaps normal would be all right.

She shook her head, tossed from left to right and back again, then sighed and turned the light back on.

There was no point entertaining these kinds of thoughts. She reached for one of the many library books she kept by her bed. Estella loved the library, even though she didn't quite understand it. They didn't charge you for books – they let you take them. But you needed a library card, which meant giving things like your name – your real name – and address. That was not something Estella could do. So she simply took the books quietly. Sometimes she even brought them back to the library when she was finished, and placed them on the shelves where they belonged. Not always, but sometimes.

She opened one book on eighteenth-century textile design, then another containing drawings of flowers.

Is this all you're destined for?

Estella winced. Of course. Cruella.

She wasn't sure when she had first known Cruella existed. That part of her had probably always been there, in the way she had grabbed for her toys in frustration and in the manner she had stomped off to school. It was Cruella who had helped her beat the bullies who tormented her. Her mum had been the one to first identify Cruella by name.

"Now what do you say to Cruella when she tries to get the better of you?" she would ask.

"Thank you for coming," Estella would reply, "but you may go now."

"Good. Now say goodbye to her."

"Goodbye, Cruella," Estella would say.

But Cruella never really went away. She took a few steps back, but she was always following, always there. Estella could hear her footsteps.

In many ways, Cruella had kept Estella alive when she arrived in London, alone and frightened. Sure, Horace and Jasper were a big part of it, but Cruella kept her going. Cruella liked taking purses and wallets. Cruella didn't care about breaking the law. Cruella wasn't disturbed by a conscience. Cruella grabbed what she needed and kept her heart hard. Estella might have cried herself to sleep many nights, but Cruella never did. Cruella kept calm and cool. Cruella survived everything.

Cruella could also be bossy and annoying. Like tonight.

She tried to bat Cruella's question away, but it floated

back into view. She was sixteen now. She might not have been going to school, but she had her natural intellect and instinct, and she had these books. She did well teaching herself. Maybe she didn't get to everything, but she knew what she needed to know. She would be just fine. When you were brilliant – and she was unquestionably brilliant – you didn't need a piece of paper to prove your worth.

She returned her focus to the drawings.

Is this all you're destined for? Making disguises? Cold spag bol? Rusty water?

Cruella again, her voice buzzing around inside of Estella's head.

"I'm not going to have to live like this forever," Estella said out loud, very quietly. "I'm going to be a designer. A famous one."

That shut Cruella up for a moment. Estella turned back to the books.

Is that all?

"Is that all?" Estella said to herself. "What else is there?"

In reply, her mind floated to the image of the couple on the grass. Not just them, but the whole group of students laughing and talking together. They were part of something more than themselves. They were *friends*.

She was part of something, too, Estella reasoned. She had Jasper and Horace and Wink and Buddy. They were all snoring away around her.

This is it? Cruella's voice pressed on. *Forever?*

"I don't know," Estella answered out loud. "I'll figure that out later."

Maybe later is now.

"Oh, very profound," she replied, a sarcastic edge to her tone, before realising that she was having this conversation with herself possibly because there was no one else to have it with.

That kind of proved Cruella's point. She fell into smug silence.

Estella shut the books angrily and went to the window, one of her favourite parts of the Lair, which had somehow survived the war and subsequent years of neglect. London was like that: so many things had taken a battering, be it from the perils of war or weather or that greatest and most constant threat, Father Time, and yet they still stood – a million beautiful little pieces of history. Things survived only to be rediscovered, revered, celebrated. Like Estella. She had survived and would keep on surviving, and the world would discover her, know her genius.

How? The answer was more work. She would make her clothes, and somehow, the clothes would take her to where she needed to be.

4

THE DULLEST GIRL IN LONDON

FEW PEOPLE regarded the teenage girl making a slow, thoughtful round of the fabric floor of Liberty of London. She wore a staid knee-length grey plaid skirt, a buttoned-up cardigan the colour of a puddle, and thick, sensible shoes that chastised the floor with their belligerent squeaks. In her arms, she clutched a massive volume called *The Book of British Birds*.

Her appearance was, of course, by design: Estella had chosen the fabrics and colours carefully, had cut the clothes in such a formless way that they dulled the senses. Estella could create clothes that made their wearer pop and seemed to dance and twirl of their own volition. And she could create clothes that made their wearer disappear. As she wandered the floor, she was insubstantial as a ghost, the embodiment of unremarkable, not worth anyone's attention.

There were few places Estella held in as high regard as the fabric department of Liberty of London. The Tudor-style store was rightly world-famous, and its architecture suggested somewhere the British royalty might live, rather than a place where one could buy home goods and clothes and jewellery.

But what set Liberty apart from every other shop was its fabric. For decades, the Liberty fabric department had produced some of the finest textiles in the world. Estella knew all the patterns, the classics and the modern, and their subtle shifts from year to year. The most delicate florals imaginable. The exquisitely complex Art Nouveau prints. The quality of the material was incomparable, the velvets thick as grass, the silks almost reflective in their sheen. The cottons were so masterfully woven that they seemed to be made of air as much as fibre.

That day, having taken an afternoon off from the boys

to indulge, she walked among the treasures, considering with a careful and unforgiving eye. She wanted something new, something that would invigorate, inspire. She would know what she needed when she saw it. She drank it in, pacing, mulling and then...

There it was: a Tana Lawn cotton in yellow dotted with an intricate pattern of pink and orange buds. Estella allowed herself a small smile and the golden feeling that washed over her when she beheld just the right fabric.

Now the real work began.

While glancing upward, seemingly engrossed in a display of tablecloths, Estella rubbed at her left sleeve like she was scratching an itch. In reality, she was sliding down a blade that was concealed there with elastic. She worked it down until it was in her grip. Then, pulling taut a few inches of the fabric from the roll, she gently made the first incision. She could have gouged the fabric, slicing off an uneven piece, but she would never do that. She treated Liberty fabric with respect. The cuts she made were perfectly straight. Even cutting blind, Estella was precise. When the first cut was made, she bent down, pretending to tie her shoe. Then... slash.

One long ribbon of fabric tumbled to the floor. She

opened her big book of birds, which was hollow inside. The fabric went in. The book was closed. The knife went back up her sleeve.

The entire process took ten seconds.

She was moving on to the next bit of fabric when she heard the girl's voice.

"This one! Richard. This one! Look at it."

Estella looked up and saw two figures at the fabric racks, not far from her. One was wearing a mini dress in a shade of orange so vibrant it caused Estella's eyes to lose focus for a moment. She wore a massive floppy brown sun hat that offset the chic dirty-blonde bob that just flirted with the nape of her neck, and a butter-yellow feather boa.

In any normal situation, she would have been the most striking person in the room, but she was equalled by the boy next to her, whose blond hair matched hers in colour and nearly in length, and who wore an impeccably tailored purple suit with a wide-striped tie in every known colour.

In addition to their hair and similarly loud, bold fashion choices, both had wide eyes and pouty lips, and their cheekbones arced through their faces at a high angle. They were virtually the same height.

"You think so?" said the one identified as Richard.

"For the downstairs, yes. But upstairs let's do something like a rainbow, don't you think? Like a rainbow that's been spilled all over a room."

Estella's first, natural instinct was to note the little Lucite handbag that hung freely from the girl's arm: she kept setting it down and walking away from it, utterly confident that no one would pick it up in Liberty. In fact, it was clear to Estella that the girl never worried about her handbag being taken from her anywhere. Such things did not occur to someone like this, and if they did occur, they would not matter. There would be another handbag, with more money inside, so why worry?

That was the kind of mark Estella preferred. But even as the handbag called to her – and it was a lovely one, a clear box with a red plastic hoop for a handle – she found that the conversation between the pair spoke to her more. She began to trail them casually. They moved around the store like it was an East End market stall. It seemed that to them, shopping for some of the finest and most expensive fabrics in London was no more consequential than purchasing potatoes.

What really held Estella's attention was their taste, which was admittedly good, though not as good as hers.

If their taste had been terrible, she would have taken the handbag and moved on. But they were so close. The crepe de chine was *almost* the right shade of pink. The floral velvet came very close to going with that brushed silk.

It was like an itch. Estella warred with herself, torn between the girl's handbag and their search for fabric. She could see a wallet inside, thick with money. Nothing would be easier. But then Richard reached up for a peacock-feather pattern in orange, and something inside Estella snapped.

"No," she heard herself say out loud. "No, not that one."

The duo turned, the girl so quickly that her massive earrings clanked and hit her in the face.

"What?" she said, her voice almost impossibly posh, her tone full of equal parts boredom and pique.

"The peacock print doesn't work with that other one you're holding," Estella continued, approaching them a bit cautiously, as one would a pair of flighty exotic animals, and delicately plucking the sample from Richard's hand. "What you want is the Ianthe print, here..."

She beckoned them to follow her to a roll of a vibrant abstract Art Nouveau pattern in bright reds, blues and golds.

"You use this one for the furniture – a settee, floor cushions. For the windows you want something like this here, this rose duchesse silk, which could be lined, or this peony vintage velvet over here..."

They followed her, silent, taking in everything she had to say. She lectured them on the heavy luxury of the brushed silk, the feline suppleness of the velvet, the dignified starch of the linen. In her mind, she assembled this room she had never seen, thinking of how the light might break through the weave of the would-be drapery and land on the soft furnishings, creating a veritable cocoon of colour and texture.

"You'd need tassels for this one, obviously," she said, regarding an abstract pattern of tangled vines. "Green ones. You could make something quite organic where it appeared that the fabric itself was—"

"Who are you?" the boy called Richard finally asked, interrupting her.

Estella jolted as though from a dream. She had forgotten herself for a moment. The plaid skirt and the knee socks. The massive book of birds tucked under her arm. The glasses.

"Estella," she replied.

"No, I mean, *who* are you? What are you doing here?"

That would not be easy to answer. What was Estella

supposed to say, that she was a girl in a costume there to steal bits of cloth and buttons? You didn't *tell* people you had come to steal; that was rule number one of stealing.

"I'm here to steal fabric," she answered plainly.

Why had she just done that?

Estella wasn't sure she knew. It was some inkling, something intangible that told her these people would like that – and she wanted these colourful, cultured people to like her.

There was a long pause, during which many things could have happened, including both of these complete strangers screaming for security to come and scoop up Estella and her book full of stolen items and pack her off to prison. And it would be absolutely deserved, because she, an idiot, had just told them she was there to steal.

As every microsecond ticked by, Estella felt something cold and unpleasant course through her veins, a growing urge to run, throw herself down the stairs, plunge through the sedate shoppers of the great Liberty, rocket out into the streets of London, and never venture there again.

"You're not," the girl said with a smile.

Estella, apparently forgetting the wave of terror and regret she had just experienced, once again went into a strange automatic movement governed not by reason but by base instinct. She cracked open the giant book and revealed the hollow interior full of buttons and swatches. Her heart was genuinely pounding like she'd just run five miles.

What was she doing?

Then the pair laughed, a bright, tinkling sound like church bells on a Sunday morning.

"I'm Magda," the girl said. She waved one manicured hand towards the boy who stood beside her. "This is Richard. And you're coming with us to the Caterpillar."

Well. That was a confusing turn.

"The what?" Estella asked.

But the two had already moved on, laughing to themselves, walking towards the lifts.

"Wait," Estella called out. "The fabric."

"We can get fabric anytime," Magda replied, looking over her shoulder. "Come on."

Estella stood for a moment in the middle of the fabric floor. A surprise confession, and now these people wanted to take her to a caterpillar? Were they police working undercover in technicolour clothing and pretending to shop for fabrics at Liberty? Was *caterpillar* the new word for *police station*?

No. No police had clothes like they were wearing. They were rare and fine – something from King's Road. These people were from a higher world of fashion than Estella had ever encountered. Nothing like them existed outside of a magazine.

The lift made a pleasant ding as it arrived on their floor.

"Are you coming?" Richard called.

Estella ran to them, her shoes protesting every inch of the way.

Outside, the sun beat down on the street, causing sweat to break out on Estella's brow. She risked a sidelong glance at Magda and Richard. They appeared as physically cool as they were socially cool. Apparently, the rich did not sweat. Perhaps they paid other people to sweat for them. Estella mopped her forehead surreptitiously and lectured herself: *No sweating, stop sweating, all sweat must cease.*

The pair proceeded down the pavement with long, confident strides and Estella half a pace behind them. They stopped a few steps in front of a Jaguar convertible. Like everything else about the two, it was brightly coloured, a peppermint green.

"In you pop," Richard said, opening the door and folding down a seat so that Estella could cram herself into the tiny space in the back.

"What do you mean by 'the caterpillar'?" Estella asked as she climbed in, none too gracefully.

"You'll see," Magda replied.

Before Estella could ask anything else, Richard hit the accelerator and pulled abruptly into traffic.

5

THE CATERPILLAR

RICHARD DROVE either very well or very poorly – or maybe both. Whatever the case, it was fast. They slipped under lights just before they changed. They took corners so tightly that Estella slid around the back of the car. All the while, Magda twiddled with the radio until she found what she deemed to be the perfect song, which she would then change ten seconds later. Her boa was flapping in the wind coming through the open window, dusting Estella's face and causing her to sneeze.

It was terrifying and exhilarating, and it was short.

This was the great advantage. With a car, you could go precisely where you wanted to go. You didn't have to take the winding bus or walk to the tube station. The city was yours to navigate as you liked. It felt powerful.

The car came to a screeching halt in some corner of Soho. Magda tripped down the pavement, feather boa flapping along behind her like the plumage of a very strange bird.

And Estella now understood what they had meant by 'the caterpillar'.

They had stopped by a place on one of the more illustrious shopping streets in the area. The entire front of the building was white – all the bricks, the windows, the stoop. On the white facade was painted a mural of the caterpillar from *Alice in Wonderland*. It was a perfect replica, with stems of grass and little Alice peering over the edge of the massive toadstool the caterpillar used as a seat. The words *The Cosmic Caterpillar* were written in a swirling orange script along the creature's back.

It was unclear where the door was, as the entire frontage was a picture. Magda seemed to know; she pushed on a spot in the base of the toadstool and it swung open.

The inside of the café was even more elaborate and otherworldly than the outside. For a start, the tables were all painted to look like spotted toadstools, and they were cut low to the ground, barely as high as Estella's knees. Instead of chairs, there were cushions scattered on the floor, which had also been painted stark white, with shades of blue projecting onto its surface, giving it the appearance of a sky with gently drifting clouds. When Estella looked up, she saw a ceiling covered in fake green grass.

Magda and Richard dropped into some cushions at a corner table and motioned for Estella to follow. Estella tried to mirror their casual positions, their forms drooping against the luxurious pillows just so, but she didn't have the support of the wall behind her. She ended up in a strange half squat, trying to look dignified as she crouched by the little toadstool. Estella felt eyes on her from around the small room. The other patrons were examining her, taking in her formless clothes and outsize book of birds.

She did not belong there. That was the vibe. In her costume, she was uncool, and the others seemed puzzled as to why Magda and Richard had brought such a person into their midst. All of this was communicated in a passing glance. The clientele at the restaurant were far too urbane to stare. They turned away, yet Estella felt their low opinions of her creeping down her spine like a small army of spiders. It was as though they could pass judgement through their stiffened and angled postures alone.

"Here you go," Magda said, sliding the menu across the table.

Estella didn't often go to places that had menus. Most times she ate at home with Jasper and Horace. They lived a life of baked beans cooked on a gas ring and unevenly toasted bread. If they were being fancy, they went to a local café for fried eggs and chips. She had no idea what most of this food even was. Quiche Lorraine? Halved avocados?

"The usual for us," Richard said casually to the server who had approached their toadstool.

"Me too," Estella said, nodding and dropping the menu. "Whatever they're having."

The server nodded and retreated, evaporating through a beaded curtain by the large mushroom on the wall.

"So," Magda said, "where are you from?"

"Oh." Estella hemmed and hawed. "Um. Up north."

"You don't sound northern," Richard replied.

"I've lived here since I was twelve," Estella said.

"For school?" Magda asked.

"School didn't really work out for me," Estella said.

"Nor us," Magda replied. "I was chucked out of Wycombe Abbey and Roedean. Richard just about made it through Winchester. I've no idea how."

Richard shrugged expansively, suggesting these things could not be known and were best left unexplored.

"So what do you do?" Estella asked.

"Do?" Magda said, her frosted pink lips forming a perfect circle around the o as her eyes widened. She and Richard burst into laughter. Estella felt a hot, sweaty discomfort come over her.

"Well," Magda said, lying back again against the cushions, after she had composed herself, "we use what our dearly departed parents left for us."

Estella felt a flicker of some old, familiar emotion on hearing those words. Maybe that was what had drawn her to those two, and what drew them to her in turn. Orphans knew their own somehow. They recognised the hard-won confidence, that veneer of self-reliance developed of need and habit, because there was no one standing behind them as support. That was how she, Jasper and Horace had found each other, after all.

"Your parents are dead?" Estella said. "I'm so sorry. My mum—"

"Don't be. They died ages ago," Magda cut in. "Car crash on holiday in Greece, when we were quite young. We barely knew them."

"Well, that's—"

"Father made his money in sweets," Magda continued breezily. "Mother came from it; her family was in construction or something dreadful like that. We got our spending dosh through a trust, and when we turned eighteen earlier this year, we got the lot. So now our job is to spend it. And we are very, very good at it."

"It's what they would have wanted," Richard joined in with a smile.

The server returned with delicate china cups of tea, bringing an end to that part of the conversation. That was probably for the best. Estella pushed the memories and feelings she'd had the sudden urge to share with the two back down deep inside, where they typically resided. She would move on, as Magda and Richard had done. That was the way. No thoughts of Mum sitting next to her, teaching her to sew. No dwelling on that night at Hellman Hall, the cold horror of seeing her mum fall...

Tea. Chin up. Drink.

Estella reached for the cup and noticed that although whatever was inside was hot and seemed tealike in consistency, it was *green*. She pulled her hand back reflexively.

Magda laughed. "Never had a green tea?" she asked with a slowly curling smile.

"I—"

"It's lovely stuff. Try it."

Estella looked around for the milk and sugar that always came with tea, but there was none to be had. Magda and Richard were drinking theirs without, so she would do the same. She lifted the cup to her lips and took a tentative sip. It wasn't bad. Drinkable, if a little grassy. The cups were real china, the kind that showed the light, and they were all mismatched: one floral, one pink with a gold rim, one a Danish blue. There was something about drinking from real china that made the tea inside taste better.

She would have liked some sugar and milk, though.

The food followed, on similarly mismatched china plates. Estella could at least work out that the main dish was something to do with eggs. There was also some sort of salad, which Estella generally did not eat. She waited for a moment, hoping that a bottle of ketchup might appear, but the Caterpillar was apparently not a ketchup sort of place.

Normally, when Estella was presented with food, she fell on it like it might try to escape from the table (which, to be fair, it might – right into Jasper's or Horace's mouth, not to mention the dogs). She went for her fork but noticed that Magda and Richard didn't even look at their plates. What were they waiting for? Estella could smell the eggs, and her stomach gurgled with want. Why didn't they eat *now*, when it was hot and fresh? Though it pained her, Estella let the food cool in front of her untasted, sipping the tea to try to squash the complaints coming from her stomach.

Magda and Richard didn't appear to be looking at anyone or anything in particular as they lounged, but Estella's practised eye saw that they were studying the room surreptitiously, exactly the same way she worked the counters of Harrods. Magda and Richard made casual conversation with other people who drifted in and out – all of them exquisitely dressed. What struck Estella was the pair's ease – the way they sometimes offered only a lazy half wave or a smirk, and things and people just seemed to orbit around them regardless.

Estella sensed that something important was happening, something she needed to embrace and make her own. These were fashionable people; it appeared fashionable people didn't pounce on their food. Fashionable people let other people come to them. They spoke when they felt like it, and they fell silent as it suited them. They lived in the kingdom that Estella hoped one day to rule with her designs. Maybe, she realised, she could follow them inside by learning the ways of the court.

But this was a lot of quiet and not eating.

"So before, you said you *both* turned eighteen?" Estella finally said, feeling the need to restart the conversation. "You're..."

"Twins." Richard nodded. "She's two minutes older."

Magda waggled her perfectly arched eyebrows. "It's why I'm so very wise."

A snort from Richard.

"I'm very much a part of the scene, you see," Magda said, as though Estella had asked her to elaborate on their circumstances. "Richard is a writer. He's working on a novel."

"Not a novel. A series of short sketches that will be loosely intertwined," he clarified.

"He hasn't started it."

"Not *yet*," he said. "I'm collecting material through living and observing."

"And you are a thief?" Magda asked, finally picking up her fork. Relieved, Estella waited a beat or two before reaching for her own.

"I steal," Estella corrected her.

Magda took a delicate bite, chewing thoughtfully. "What's the difference?" she asked once she'd swallowed.

For Estella, this was absolutely clear. *Thief* was a definitive term – the sum total of who a person was. Taking things that belonged to others wasn't who Estella was; it was just what she did to get by, to fund her true calling. She stole food, or she stole money to buy food. She stole fabric to make her clothes. And sure, they stole the occasional item here or there to make the Lair a bit nicer, but that was simply a way of making their burned-out hovel into a home. Birds weren't considered thieves just because they took what they needed to make their nests, were they?

So Estella stole, yes, but she was not a thief.

All of this was straightforward enough to Estella, but she was unsure how to even begin explaining it to Magda and Richard. How could she put the value of money into words for people who had never been without it? How could she talk about the hunger that woke her up sometimes at night – how it hurt so much that she shook from it? Watching Magda and Richard pick at their food, Estella could see they wouldn't have a clue.

Estella suddenly felt a bit miserable. That was sometimes the cruellest thing of all about poverty: it could make one feel small, almost embarrassed. There was no reason for it. It wasn't her fault. It didn't mean she was any less of a person. But there it was, that creeping dread of humiliation.

Luckily for Estella, Richard swept the conversation along.

"Why bits of cloth? They can't be worth much. Don't you... sell it or something?" He took a dignified sip of tea. "Market stalls under the cover of darkness? Dirty deeds in the East End with people with exciting names? Tony the Hammer or Razor Jim?"

Magda laughed. "Are you a gangster?" she asked. "Oh, I do hope so."

"No," Estella said. "I take the cloth to... make things. I design clothes."

That got a laugh of disbelief from both of her companions. Its ripples echoed around the room, drawing the attention of the languid people at the other tables. Estella had a sinking sensation in the pit of her stomach.

They laugh? At you? Unacceptable.

Go away, Cruella.

But Cruella did have a point. It was impossible for Estella to back down from a challenge, especially one involving clothing. If this was a test, she would pass with flying colours. She would impress these unimpressible people, and she would do it to let them know she was a force of fashion to be reckoned with and respected.

"I'll be back in a moment," she said, setting her fork down carefully on the side of the plate.

Magda and Richard looked up in surprise as she left the table and the restaurant.

Estella needed something fast, disposable. She needed immediacy. She glanced up and down the street. On the far corner, there was a man selling some newspapers at a stall.

Newspapers.

She raced to the newspaper man, digging around in her pocket for whatever money she had there. "Five *Evening Standard*s," she said, slapping the coins into his palm and snatching up the papers. "Or whatever you've got. I don't care."

Estella found the closest of Soho's many alleyways. This one was too narrow for cars, so it was suitable for her purposes. She flattened the papers on the ground. She needed something simple. She had seen people in paper dresses before. A simple A-line.

She could do a bit better than that.

She slapped down her *Book of British Birds* and opened it, then looked through the materials inside. A shape appeared in her mind. Paper was quite easy to work with; that was how she made patterns, after all. This time, she would simply wear the pattern.

Estella drew out her knife (perhaps she was Razor Jim after all) and slashed through the newspaper. Some of the cuts were long, making the basic outlines of the piece. From there, she made the more delicate ones, nips and tucks and places where the tabs would come together.

As she worked, a boy turned down the alley on a motor scooter.

"Hey!" he said. "Out of the way! I'm trying to get through here!"

"Well, you're not," Estella replied, keeping her eyes trained on her work.

"You can't just—"

"Go. Round."

She flashed the driver a rude gesture. He gave a similarly

rude reply before walking his scooter back out of the mouth of the alley and onto the street.

Estella dug around in the contents of the book and found a length of blue edging ribbon she had taken earlier in the day. She sliced it in two and used it to lace together the two sides of the dress.

Practised at making quick changes in various dark and empty corners of London, Estella deftly removed her cardigan and skirt and slid the delicate paper outfit over her head. It made quite a lot of noise for a dress, and it wasn't the most comfortable item, but it fit well. Estella knew her sizes. She adjusted some of the folds and tightened the lacing on the sides.

The Estella who re-entered the Cosmic Caterpillar was far different from the one who had appeared before. This time, dressed in her new creation, she felt confident. And when every eye fell on her, the expressions were different.

They were interested now. They were impressed.

"I knew it!" Magda said as Estella sauntered back to their toadstool, unable to stop a smile tugging at her lips. "She's magic! I told you, Richard. You know I have a sense for these things."

Estella noted that her plate was gone. She had barely

eaten a thing. That was a blow, but not a monumental one. What mattered most was the dress. She had won the day with the dress.

"What should we call her?" Magda asked her brother. "Essie? Stella?"

"Stellar, I think," Richard replied.

"Stellar! That's very good."

The server returned with bowls of ice cream, which she set ceremoniously in front of them.

"Oooh, they have honey and ginger root today," Magda cooed. "My favourite."

Estella didn't know what ginger root was, but honey was delicious, and how could ice cream be anything other than good? This time, she did not wait. She picked hers up and ate it with relish, while Richard and Magda took only a few spoonfuls before letting the rest melt.

The music piped in through the restaurant's speakers switched songs, and Estella recognised it at once: it was "Everybody's Sun", from that band with the ridiculous name she'd heard the students squealing over in Hyde Park the other day. The now-familiar words washed over her like a warm bath:

Over the city, it's coming down
Day is done for London town
Rises up and wants its tea
Eggs and beans and hot coffee

It's everybody's sunrise
That's when the day starts
It's everybody's sunset
Just where the day parts
Everybody's sun
It belongs to everyone

"I love this song," Estella said.

"You like the Electric Teacup?" Magda asked.

Estella gulped. Was that a bad thing? If so, it was too late. She'd committed. She nodded.

"You have good taste," Magda said. "They're going to be all the rage soon. In fact, there's going to be a party for them tomorrow night, to celebrate their new album. You should come."

"To a party?" Estella said, barking out a laugh. "For them? Me?"

Her utter uncoolness sizzled over the table for a moment. She shook her head sharply to bring herself back.

"I may be able to carve out some time tomorrow," she said, trying again, making her voice slow and casual.

"Here." Magda ripped a corner off Estella's dress and scrawled an address in pencil. "It's on Oakley Street, just off King's Road."

"We should go," Richard announced, stifling a yawn.

Magda grabbed her boa and tossed it back around her neck; then she and Richard stood and went straight for the door. Estella had done more than one runner after eating, but this place seemed different. The server knew them, and there was clearly no problem in terms of money. She wavered, unsure of whether to leave. Was she supposed to pay?

The server looked at Estella, who was staring at Magda's and Richard's retreating backs.

"They come here almost every day," the server, having noticed Estella's confusion, whispered to her. "We just send them the bill once a month."

Estella felt her cheeks flush slightly. "Right. Of course. I know. I was just looking for my..." She had nothing with her but her book and her bundle of clothes, which she pointed to lamely. "Oh, I have them. Thank you."

Outside, normal London seemed strange. The sky was back in its customary position. The grey stone and cream paint and black wrought iron railings seemed quaint, like set dressings, after the restaurant's and her companions' explosions of colour.

Richard was already behind the wheel of his car; Magda was settling herself in the passenger seat. "The party tomorrow starts at nine," she called out to Estella through the open window, "but no one will be there until ten or so. Wear something stunning. Show us what you can do."

With that, the car peeled away, leaving Estella standing in front of the Caterpillar, wondering what had just happened to her.

6

THE BOY IN
THE KITCHEN

EſTELLA ARRIVED home to find Horace hanging halfway out the window and Jasper balancing on one foot, holding one television antenna close to the ground while pushing the other away with his suspended leg.

"How about now?" Jasper asked.

"Down. No. Other one. Down. No. Up."

"Which is it?" Jasper asked.

"The down one needs to go up and the up one needs to go down. Oh, Stel's here."

"Thank god," Jasper said as he tumbled to the floor. "Footy's on. You do the antenna. Horace is going to keep watch out the window for the detector van for the first half and I'll do the second."

The trio had found their television in a house where the windows were left open far too frequently, and as everyone knew, if you left a window open, the television might blow away. The problem was, of course, that to operate your television, you needed a licence. The BBC was very serious about it. They had a detector van that drove around, looking for stolen signals. Every time the telly was on, there was the risk of discovery. In the Lair, whenever someone wanted to watch, one person would work the antenna to try to get reception, and another would be the lookout and yell at the first sign of any strange, lingering vans.

It was exhausting, and the reception was bad, but still. Telly.

"I can't," Estella answered, a little breathless as she hurried to her sewing table.

"Why?" Horace asked.

"Are you wearing a newspaper?" Jasper added, an incredulous note in his voice.

"Yes. And I need to finish this dress by tomorrow."

"Why?" Jasper asked.

Estella had never had any secrets from Horace and Jasper. There had never been anything to conceal. Oddly, however, she found she didn't really want to tell them about her afternoon, about the possibilities it held for her if she played the next step very, very carefully.

But she had no other explanation to offer. She had to tell them.

"I'm going to a party."

"A party?" Jasper repeated as he climbed into the hammock. "I like parties. Where are we going?"

"Er... not you," Estella clarified. "Me. I've been invited."

"Invited?"

"Whose party is this?" Horace said.

"Some people I met," Estella said, forcing her tone to remain casual and breezy. "At Liberty."

"Some marks?" Horace asked.

"Not marks," Estella said. "People."

"Marks," Jasper repeated.

"No." Estella shook her head. "People. Nice people. They took me to the Caterpillar—"

"The what?" Jasper said. "Stel, are you feeling all right?"

"It's a café. I had an omelette – I think. And they asked me to go to a party, and I want to go. And I need a fabulous dress to wear, so..." Estella's voice trailed off as she gestured towards her sewing machine.

The boys took this in for a moment, Horace still entangled in the television aerials and Jasper ticking back and forth in the hammock.

"What's an omelette?" Horace finally asked.

"And we are your guests at this party," Jasper added. "Right? These nice people, no reason we shouldn't meet them and their wallets."

"No," she said, and bit her lower lip in frustration. "Just... Quiet. I need to concentrate."

Jasper and Horace fell silent, but they both watched her as she guided the scissors into the fabric. The sound, the tiny snick as the scissors separated the fibres, echoed around the Lair. It was hard to work with them breathing down her neck, staring at her.

"You're going to go to this party without us?" Horace said.

Jasper and Horace didn't look hurt, exactly; it was more confusion that was slowly making its way towards hurt.

"It's a thing... a thing with clothes," she sputtered. "That's why I need the dress."

The boys visibly and immediately relaxed. "Why didn't you just say so?" Horace said as he returned to the business of the television, working its aerials once again.

It was true enough. In fact, it was *entirely* true, now that she thought about it. This was about clothes, about fabric, about fashion. Yes, it was a party for a band – a famous band – and yes, Jasper and Horace would probably like to go to a party for a famous band. But it all had to do with the clothes and the fabric, with what she would see other people wearing and what people would see on her. So it was fine not to take them. Fine.

Estella opened her *Book of British Birds* and removed the fabric she had taken that afternoon from Liberty. She examined the cloth, feeling it under her fingers. She studied the pattern, the way it moved. Her mind drew the line through it, carefully retaining the printed design as it sketched her new, larger design on top. Buddy curled up on her feet as she carefully added the last bits to the design. She had intended to work on the dress for weeks more when the vision had first taken shape for her in Liberty, but it was needed now. Her fingers moved faster and faster until they were a blur of activity. Every ounce of her concentration was focused on the task at hand.

The following evening, just as the sky was starting to darken, it was done.

Estella lifted it gently from the table and took it behind the screen to try on. It fit superbly. She looked down at the cluster of blossoms she had created, the vines that ran down her arms and ended in pink and orange buds around the wrists. When she stepped out from behind the screen, Jasper and Horace, who were trying to work the aerials and the detector van watch by themselves, did not notice.

She cleared her throat.

"That's amazing," Jasper said as Estella twirled around.

"You look like... a girl," Horace added.

Estella understood.

"Well, if there's nice food, you're going to bring us some, right?" Horace squinted at her.

"Yes," she said. "Yes, of course. Yes."

She finished getting ready, brushing out her hair, trying it up and down and up again before leaving it long and straight. She did her makeup quickly, lining her eyes with dark kohl. She stepped back and, turning from side to side, reviewed herself in their chipped mirror. The dress really was all that she had hoped it would be. It somehow flowed yet hugged the body at the same time, in just the right way. It was mini, but not overly so. Anyone could cut a mini; she wanted the hem of this dress to catch the wind, to sway as she danced.

If she danced.

As she stepped outside into the warm evening, she felt a flicker of guilt about her lie.

She looked up at the patchwork building that was their home. Patchwork building, patchwork dress, patchwork life... No.

This was about her skill and the right people seeing her work. This was about her taking advantage and making the most of a business opportunity, pure and simple.

And besides, only she had been invited.

Chelsea, where Oakley Street was located, was not that far from where Estella and Jasper and Horace lived – two bus rides away, or a fairly quick trip on the tube.

Socially, however, it might as well have been on another planet. There were no market stalls there, no people selling scrap on the street. If buildings had been bombed there, they had been repaired in a timely manner. Many of the stately dwellings had stood for hundreds of years and had been home to poets and scientists and writers and explorers. The grass was greener, because there *was* grass. The Thames was only a stone's throw away. This was the London the tourists came to see, with the black cabs circling around and the bright red pillar-box phone booths (which they had in Estella's area as well, only much grimier, with glass panes covered in dirty adverts).

The address she had been given was on a quiet residential street of sombre homes, and it was immediately clear which house the party was in. Estella could see all the lights in the house were on behind the curtains of many colours that obscured the inside. The entire structure throbbed gently with music.

For a moment, standing on the pavement in front of the gate, she considered running away. *Silly,* she scolded herself. Estella ran from nothing, except the occasional police officer. Certainly not from fancy houses. She took a deep, steadying breath. She was crossing into something she wanted and didn't really understand. There was something in this house she needed.

Estella knocked on the door. No reply. Just the beat

of the music and the muffled sound of voices came from within. She tried the doorknob and the door opened. As she stepped inside, she reeled from the cloud of incense that hit her face. The air was tinted by it. Her eyes watered and she coughed for several seconds before she made her way further in.

The hall was dimly lit by a brass lamp that hung from the ceiling and sent out soft beams of purple and red through coloured panes of glass. It was clear that many people were inside the house, but none were in immediate view except for a girl in a pair of orange harem pants with a matching halter top and a daisy painted on her cheek. She did a snaking dance in the middle of the hall all by herself, her eyes closed in pleasure.

Estella would have to go deeper into the house, clearly. When she tried to edge past Harem Pants, the girl suddenly stopped dancing and looked at her.

"Ginger!" she said, lurching forward and touching Estella's brassy red hair. "Hello, ginger, hello. Hello, ginger."

"Hello," Estella replied.

"There's a party, you know," the girl said, leaning in conspiratorially.

"Yes," Estella said. "That's why I'm here."

"I've been here for a while." The girl resumed some of her snaking arm motions, watching her own movements with fascination. "Maybe I've always been here."

"I'm just going to go inside," Estella said.

But the girl was not done. She slid closer to Estella and whispered into her ear. "I can speak to flowers." She pointed to the daisy on her cheek.

"That's nice."

"They speak to me as well," the girl went on, "but only sometimes. Hydrangeas, mostly. But I did meet a peony the other day that told me a secret."

Estella nodded and tried to press past gently.

"The purple ones say the most," the girl whispered to her. "The blue ones always lie."

"I'll bear that in mind," Estella said.

The girl seemed satisfied now that she had imparted that information. She turned away and began to crawl up the stairs on her hands and knees.

Estella made her way deeper into the house, through the ever-thickening clouds of incense and tinted half-light. There were more people now, in all sorts of velvets and silks and little metallic mini dresses. It was impossible to tell whose house it was. It was simply dark and full and loud. Clumps of people – all of them looking ever so cool – were congregating in corners together or lounging on cushions. It was one thing to see clothes like the ones they were wearing in the shop windows or in an advert. It was entirely another to see the outfits in the habitat for which they were intended. These were the people who *wore* fashion.

It was like stepping into a magazine. There was an Ossie Clark dress, perfectly fitted and flowing like water. There was a Mary Quant, short and crisp. Estella clocked it all, every pattern, every cut. And the makeup was unlike anything Estella had seen up close. There were mustard yellow eye shadows, twinkling face jewels, mad drawings done in face crayon and eyeliner. The partygoers wore feathers around their necks, silver bands in their hair. Their feet were adorned with extravagant slippers and platform boots. It was a wonderland.

What other people were wearing, that was all well and good. But Estella hadn't come only to look at other people's clothes. *Her* dress was what mattered. Her dress was her passport into this world. The reaction was subtle, as it would be among that crowd, but she saw people eyeing it – and her – approvingly. They didn't say anything or proffer a smile, but they moved gently out of the way to make room for her, wordlessly accepting her as one of their own. She pressed further in, through progressively darker rooms, until she found one that was almost blacked out from all the scarves that had been put over the lights.

After several minutes of weaving through the mass of people, Estella finally spotted Richard and Magda lounging on a sofa. There was a guy pressed into Magda's side; he played idly with the tips of her short hair.

"Darrrrrling," Magda said, stretching out an elegant arm, her hand hanging limp like a heavy flower head on a strong stalk. Somehow, she made that one word last for what seemed like a full minute, and she conveyed so much with that word alone: a life of confidence, comfort and certainty.

In short, a life of money.

"Look at your dress!" Magda exclaimed. "Did you make that as well?"

Estella nodded.

"Sit!"

Estella dallied awkwardly on the fringe of the group, trying to figure out where to place herself. Despite Magda's indicating she should join them, no one in the small group actually made room for Estella to seat herself. There wasn't quite enough space on the sofa for her where they were positioned. She thought about perching on the arm of the sofa, though one member of the party had an elbow on it and didn't seem inclined to move. There was a tiny bit of space, maybe enough for half a person. Estella decided to go for it, perching on the edge and gently pressing herself back until the girl next to her finally adjusted her elbow, looking as though it pained her greatly to do so.

"This is Michael," Magda said, motioning to the guy who continued to toy with her hair. He seemed utterly absorbed by it. She reached for him, put her hand gently around his chin, and kissed him.

Estella waved at Michael, who appeared too preoccupied by Magda to return the gesture.

"There was a girl in the hall who said she could talk to flowers before she crawled up the stairs," Estella said.

"Oh, that's Gogo," Magda said, laughing lightly. "She's away with the proverbial, you know? Perhaps a little too much sunshine."

Estella did not know, but she nodded. The only way she would manage this – the only way to learn what she needed to know – was to fake it for a bit. Lots of nodding and mental notes. The way everyone leaned back on one elbow, with their feet casually tucked under them. The close, casual way they draped against one another.

Michael began chewing the ends of Magda's hair, which Magda did not seem to notice.

"It's all a bit dreadful," Magda said, indicating the room and everyone in it, "but not so bad."

Casual introductions were made. There was a Penelope, a Roger, a Jane, a Max, a Felicity. No real effort was made to pin down which of these people were connected to which names, each one introduced with a careless flick of the wrist, and then Magda kept right on with the conversation, absolutely none of which Estella could follow.

"There's going to be an opening at Revolution," Magda said. "For Apple."

"I saw the Fool the other day outside Mr Fish," the one who might have been Penelope replied.

"They're doing Savile Row, you know."

Estella tried not to let her expression betray her total confusion. Occasionally, one or two people got up and danced. Mostly, though, it was conversation and long, cool looks around the room. Estella had nothing to offer by way of the former, but the latter she could do.

She concentrated on trying to look both disinterested and engaged at the same time but found it hard to focus on her expression with the pungency of the incense that seemed to be coming from every direction, tickling her nose and throat. She pressed the cough down, but her throat was unbearably dry. She glanced around and saw that some people had drinks. They had to come from somewhere. If she didn't get something to drink, she was going to start hacking in a way that would be irredeemable. She gave a big sniff. It seemed her nose was now getting in on the action as well, and that just would not do. Not among this crowd.

"Excuse me," she said, lifting herself as casually as she could manage. "I think I see someone I know."

It was difficult to keep the impending sneeze at bay, but she managed as she made her way back and peered into every room until she came to what appeared to be the kitchen.

She ducked inside just before bursting into a sneezing fit. She had never sneezed quite like that – an explosive, repetitive frenzy. A machine gun of sneeze. Her body seemed to want to fling the incense as far away from her nasal passages as it could. Estella blinked and staggered for a moment when it was over.

Then someone began to clap.

She heard a voice. "That was amazing. Do it again."

There was someone in the dim room. She could make out that it was a boy, perhaps her age. By the pale light of the kitchen window, she could see he was perhaps the least colourfully dressed person in the house, in a simple pair of brown trousers and an off-white shirt. He'd made a bit of an effort with a scarf, also brown, he had tied around his neck. A shame he was dressed so plainly, because on further inspection Estella found him to be quite good-looking. His face was almost heart-shaped; he had a widow's peak, and from there, his face narrowed down to a bit of a pointed chin. His hair was a dusty blond, roughly cut and grazing his neckline.

He was holding on to the handle of a kettle like it might try to get away from him.

"Don't stop on my account," he continued as he set the kettle on the base. "Wish I'd recorded that. I could use that for something."

Estella couldn't see a smile, but she could hear it in his voice. She straightened herself up and found some glasses that had been stacked on a table. She grabbed one, marched to the sink and filled the glass with lukewarm water, which she drank greedily. A trickle ran down her chin.

"Thirsty," the boy observed. "Not used to the atmosphere?"

"The incense may be too much."

"It stinks," he said plainly. "People seem to like it, but I hate it."

The kettle whistled, and he took it off the base and filled his cup.

"Like a cuppa?" he asked.

"No, thank you."

"I'm the only person around here drinking any tea tonight," he said. "I suppose one of us has to."

"Why?" Estella said.

The boy squinted at her as though she might be a bit slow. "One of us," he said again.

"But why?"

"It's in the name," he said, sounding puzzled. "The Electric Teacup?"

"Oh," Estella said. "The band. Sure. Are they here yet?"

"Well, I am."

It took Estella a beat before it clicked.

"Oh," she said, embarrassed. "Oh. You're in—"

"I am indeed."

"Oh. I'm sorry." Estella felt herself flushing. She should

have done her homework on the band before going to a party in their honour.

But the boy seemed the furthest thing from offended, offering Estella a sloping grin. "Nothing to be sorry for," he said, bobbing the tea bag by the string before removing it and setting it on a plate. "You're not to know what we all look like. I think the others are running late. You'll know when Chris gets here, though, because the whole place will go mad. Chris is the singer." He half smiled, half grimaced. "You'll see. Mad."

"But why are you in here?" Estella said. "This is your party. For all of you."

The boy shook his head. "I don't know who owns this place. I was given an address and told to come, so I did. I was in the sitting room for a while, listening to people talk. Thing is, I've no idea what they're on about. Got bored. Came in to make a cup of tea."

He stirred the tea. Then he crashed around a bit, looking for the sugar and milk.

"I'm the boring one. Reliable, though." He smirked and tapped his chest. "Like Bow Bells, that's me."

"So you don't like this kind of thing," Estella said.

"It's bleeding awful. I'll go home in a bit, listen to music and play my guitar. But they tell me stick my face in, so the face gets stuck. I take it from the fact that you're hiding in here at the sink that you don't like it much, either. How did you end up here?"

"I was invited," Estella said simply. "So I came. I don't get invited to many parties."

"Lucky," he said. "What's your name?"

"Estella."

"I'm Peter. Nice to make your acquaintance."

Suddenly, there was tremendous noise in the hall and a cheer that rose up and around.

"Dear oh dear," Peter murmured. "That'll be the others arriving. Chris is certainly here. I told you. Everything goes mad when Chris is around."

The clatter came down the hallway – lots of loud male voices and someone with a window-shaking laugh.

"Peter!" the person shouted. "Pe-ter!"

Peter sighed and pushed himself away from the counter.

"In here!" he called.

A guy appeared in the doorway. Even in the dim hallway light, Estella could make out that he was handsome, with great valleys under the mighty peaks of his cheekbones and flowing dark hair. His voice had a husky rasp she recognised from "Everybody's Sun"; he was the singer for certain.

He cocked his hip, owning the doorway. "What are you doing in here?" he asked.

"Drinking tea," Peter said. "Talking. Plotting a series of murders, if you must know."

"Time to be social. People want to meet you. Stop lurking in the shadows. Shift it."

Suddenly, Chris seemed to notice that Estella was there. "Oh," he said. "Sorry, love. But we need him. Come on, Pete."

"Yeah," Peter replied. "In a minute."

"You be careful with this one," Chris said to Estella, smiling. "He's trouble." Then Chris detached himself from the doorway and vanished into the party.

"Should I not have mentioned the murders?" Peter asked in a mock-concerned tone. "I keep doing that. Anyway, that is Chris. He wears the tight trousers, and ten people will fall in love with him tonight. He's a good singer, though, so we keep him. Anyway, I'd better go out. The show must go on."

As Peter started to make his way out of the room, he picked up something from the counter and handed it to her. It was the band's record album.

"Here you go," he said. "Compliments of the management. Enjoy in good health."

Estella stood for a moment in the empty kitchen, clutching the album to her chest.

7

A LITTLE SHOPPING

THE BOYS were both long asleep – Horace in his bed, Jasper in the hammock – by the time Estella returned to the Lair later that night. Their snoring filled the hot air. She took off her shoes and crept across the creaking floor, stopping to give Wink a scratch on the head. She looked around, perceiving the Lair anew in light of the opulence and extravagance she had just experienced – and she didn't like what she saw. Or smelled. The space was laden with overtones of mildew, hints of beans and other, less appetising odours. She was overcome by a sense of profound dissatisfaction, which only increased as she crossed the room silently, shoes in hand.

When Estella reached her sectioned-off corner, an anxious Buddy jumped up to greet her and pace around. He licked her hands and legs, jumping onto and off the bed. He was unused to her being out by herself so late.

"It's okay," she whispered to him, rubbing his ears. "I was at a party."

He sniffed her hair hard, then sneezed in her face.

She set the album down on her pillow, then removed her dress carefully and hung it by the window to air out. After washing her face in cold, rusty water, she climbed into bed, where she tossed and turned and eventually kicked away the covers and looked out the large round window, reflecting on her evening like one waking from a lurid, thrilling dream.

And it had been very much like a dream, from the singularly odd Gogo to Estella's unexpected exchange with Peter in the dimly lit kitchen. Magda and Richard had taken their leave shortly after the Electric Teacup had begun to play, parting with another invitation to Estella to join them at the Caterpillar the next day. "Wear another one of your amazing creations," Magda had said before blowing Estella a goodbye kiss.

Estella tried to get comfortable. The beds in that house where the party had been must have had lovely, smooth sheets, she thought. Cool, crisp, laundered and pressed regularly. Estella's sheets had come from a market stall. They were itchy and thin and tore if you looked at them the wrong way. (She was perfectly capable of making a sheet, but artists like Estella didn't cut and sew for no reason. Sheets were not a creation. They were just rectangles.)

Frustrated, Estella pulled the Electric Teacup album to her and studied the sleeve. The cover of the album was a photo of the four members of the band in a garden, posed as if they were having a tea party. Chris was prominently featured. He sat closest to the camera and had his arm extended, holding out a teacup, as though offering it to his myriad admirers. All cheekbones and thick dark hair, he was exceedingly handsome, in an obvious way. But Peter – there was a sharpness to him. He stood in the back, behind the others, holding his teacup and smirking gently.

She flipped the album over and read the song titles and notes. Every song was credited to Peter Perceval. Music and lyrics. And then, as she glanced over who was playing what instruments, she noticed that once again, Peter seemed to be doing the majority of the work. Guitar, piano, organ, mellotron, harmonica...

"So why aren't you the famous one," Estella wondered aloud to the album, "if you're doing all the work?"

She placed the album on her rickety bedside table and looked at the ceiling.

Wear another one of your amazing creations.

Her dress had been her showstopper. Of course she had other outfits, but none that seemed quite right. If she wanted Magda, Richard and the others to take her seriously as a designer, enough so that she could cement her place in this new world, she was going to have to come up with something.

She closed her eyes and tried to recall everything she had seen that evening – every material, colour and texture. Metallics, velvets, silk scarves, feathers... so many things had already been used. What did she have that was different?

What would Peter like?

That was an unexpected thought. What did she care what Peter would like? He was just a boy having a cup of tea at a party. Besides, there was no guarantee she would ever see him again, let alone at the Caterpillar.

Yet the thought also provided a bit of an answer. Peter

would like something unusual, something clever. They had met in a kitchen. What if she did an outfit that was somehow kitchen-based? The mundane and ordinary made spectacular and amusing.

It came to her all at once just as her eyelids grew heavy.

Before anyone else at the Lair was awake the next morning, Estella had been out to the shops. Four of them, to be exact.

A tall pyramid of Heinz baked beans tins, all with labels removed, balanced on the table. Estella was on the floor by her sewing table, digging through one of her many boxes of materials and scraps. Dozens of Heinz baked beans labels were scattered around her on the floor.

"What are you doing?" Jasper asked, scuffing up with his big bare feet.

"I got you some beans," she replied.

"You got us *all* of the beans. Why?"

There. She finally found what she was looking for. "This," she announced, holding aloft like a trophy two clear rain slickers from the bottom of one of the boxes.

"What?"

Jasper's questions were going unanswered, so he gave up and went to switch on the kettle.

"How was your party?" he asked a moment later.

"What?" Estella ripped the packages open and spread the slickers out on the ground. "Oh. Fine."

"Any good angles to work?"

"What? Yes. Later."

Horace woke up then, rubbing the sleep from his eyes as he stared in confusion at the shiny pyramid of unlabelled tins on the table.

"What's all this?" he asked.

"Estella bought some beans," Jasper said.

"How'd you know they're beans?"

"She took the labels off."

"Why?" Horace asked.

Jasper shrugged.

"If we put them with the other tins, how will we know which ones are beans? Hey, Stel, how will we—"

"Because they'll be the tins with no labels," Estella snapped through a mouthful of pins as she crawled around the slickers, marking lines.

"What if the label comes off another tin?"

"I'm trying to work," she said, exasperated.

Jasper and Horace exchanged knowing looks. When Estella used *that* tone, it was time to back away quietly.

Estella rummaged around until she procured thick, heavy needles to work with the plastic. It was a long, hot hour at the sewing machine, but when she lifted her head, her new creation was ready: a clear plastic dress lined with pocket space on the inside. In this case, the pockets were not for stolen goods; they were sleeves for the bean tin labels. She slid the labels in, one by one, making sure the pattern was correct, as Jasper and Horace watched, utterly bemused.

At last, Estella stepped behind her screen and emerged in her new creation.

"Well?" she asked them.

"It's a baked beans dress," Horace said slowly, stating the obvious.

"But how does it look?"

"Like beans," he said. "I don't get it."

"It's art," she explained. "Like Andy Warhol and the tomato soup."

"Andy who? What about soup?"

"What's the angle?" Jasper asked from a safe place across the room. "Are you going to do a run at a greengrocer or something?"

"It's not an angle. It's fashion."

"If you say so, Stel," Jasper replied. "Looks like a bunch of bean tin labels to me, but you're the one who knows."

"You're correct, I am the one who knows," Estella replied. She blew out a breath, annoyed. There wasn't enough time in the world to explain fashion to Jasper and Horace. She'd once taken the better part of an afternoon convincing them that you had to wear matching shoes, even if they were "both black, well, kind of, this one's brown but I put black polish on it."

Besides, you didn't explain fashion. You knew it when you saw it. It was understood. You didn't need to be told why Vionnet's bias cut worked so well, or why Elsa Schiaparelli's putting a lobster on a dress was genius. It simply *was*.

"Well, I'm going out," Estella announced.

"Where to now?" Jasper asked.

"It's more of the same stuff," she said evasively.

"Well, at some point you have to explain what the angle is. You'll be back in time for us to do a run today, yeah? Bank holiday weekend."

"Sure," Estella said, not really paying attention as she scrutinised her face in the cracked, dusty mirror.

"When?"

"I don't know... around four?"

She didn't mean to be so dismissive, and she was sure they knew that. Horace and Jasper were so much a part of her life – of her – that explanations were not required. Besides, this particular new venture of Estella's was difficult to explain, because the boys only saw things in terms of immediate gain. Wallets. Watches. Food. They didn't think about intangible goals, long-term plans. They let Estella do that kind of tactical thinking for them. Estella advanced their game, improved their living conditions, looked around the corner for the next destination. They were lovable, but they had no vision. As far as they were concerned, it would be the three of them, up there in the Lair, forever. And as much as she adored them, the thought of that cut her breathing short.

Estella refocused her attention on her reflection in the mirror. This time, she would be better prepared for the Caterpillar. She fine-tuned her makeup based on some things she had seen the night before. Estella had loads of makeup to work with, as she scooped it up by the bagful from Woolworths at every opportunity. A quick swipe of eyeliner on the inner crease of the lid. A mix of pink and white on the lips. White shadow mixed with a baby blue. A little white shadow high on the cheekbones as well.

When Estella was satisfied, she had a final check of the bean dress in the mirror, waved to Jasper and Horace and headed out once again, back to her new Soho hangout.

Estella arrived at the Caterpillar early, by almost a full half hour, but didn't want to be seen doing so. She knew enough about the fashionable set to know late was on time. Early was just sad. Early lost the game.

She wandered up the street and around the corner and back again, repeating the process until she was sure to be at least fifteen minutes late. One thing she noted: the plastic dress was hot. Very hot. Sweat poured down her back and legs. The bright side was no sweat marks.

When she saw Magda and Richard's Jaguar pull down the street, she ducked behind a postbox, emerging only when a woman came to drop a letter and jumped back with a startled yelp at the sight of a girl dressed as a tin of beans – or several tins of beans – squatting nearby. Estella sprang up and strode towards the Caterpillar as if nothing out of the ordinary had occurred. This was Swinging London, after all. People were bound to squat behind postboxes and spring out from time to time.

She waited long enough to be sure that Magda and Richard would be seated and ready to take in her entrance. She found them sitting at the same table they had occupied two days before. Magda's face broke into a smile as Estella entered.

"What a gas!" Magda said upon seeing her. "An absolute gas!" She nudged her brother. "Richard, do you see?"

Richard saw, of course, and nodded distractedly. He had a book of poetry in front of him.

Magda rose from her low-slung seat and walked all the way around Estella, taking in the bean dress from every angle.

"A gas," she said again. "I love it."

Estella allowed herself one small, unimpressed smile, as though this were praise that was heaped upon her all the time, and then sat down with them. This time, she made an effort not to stare at the clouds on the floor or the grass on the ceiling or any of the outfits or people. *Look bored.* She tipped up her chin the way Magda held hers. Regal. That was what it was.

Their server that day was wearing a simple and elegant white mini shift dress with tiny bells along the hem. They tinkled gently against her mid thighs as she walked. Estella did minute calculations in her mind regarding the precise length of the skirt. Five inches above the knee. Straight cut.

"Same?" the server asked.

"Same," Magda said.

"Same," Richard said.

Estella blanked for only a moment before saying, "Same."

The server tinkled away and through the beaded curtain. The music played low and soft, and everyone eased back onto the cushions.

"So what did you think of last night?" Magda asked Estella.

"I liked it. A lot."

"It was all right, wasn't it? Not too terribly dreadful. Everyone thought you were a gas. An absolute gas."

Estella noticed Magda was saying that word a lot that day. She had not said it the day before. What did it mean when she repeated that word? Was repetition in vogue now?

"You were talking to Peter for a while," Magda observed.

"Oh, we just happened to meet while he was... making tea," Estella replied, a bit lamely, flattered and surprised that Magda had noticed.

Magda smiled knowingly. "He's rather something, isn't he? You know they're going to be massive, absolutely massive. Everyone's saying so."

The cups of green tea arrived, and this time, Estella didn't look the slightest bit surprised by the colour. The grassy liquid would never replace her cuppa, but it wasn't bad. She could get used to it.

Richard was in a chatty mood after he put down his poetry book. "I'm working on a new idea," he said. "A sort of Joycean-inspired process, but I've been thinking a lot about Burroughs, and what I'm really aiming to do is combine those two basic processes into one process, if you see what I mean." He had a habit of drawing out his words and pulling lightly on his chin as if he had a beard, which he did not.

"Sounds marvellous," Magda said. Estella nodded in agreement, though she had no clue what he was talking about.

The server brought the same meal as they'd had two days earlier. Magda and Richard picked at theirs as they dissected all the people and things they'd seen the night before. Who was with whom, who was wearing what, who hadn't shown.

"I thought today we might do a bit of clothes shopping," Magda said as the dishes were cleared away.

The plastic dress squeaked on the seat. It was like a rain forest inside. Plastic did not breathe.

"Oh," Estella said. "I'm not sure... I've got to be somewhere..."

Magda flicked her hand as though waving away Estella's protests. "Surely you can spare the time. We'll only go for a moment. You're so wonderful with clothes, I'd just love to shop with you. Don't you want everyone to see your fabulous dress?"

Those were the words Estella needed to hear. She had no greater desire than for people to see her dresses. She didn't really have to be home, she reasoned to herself. They could do a run anytime. Jasper and Horace could wait.

"Of course," Estella said with a warm smile. "Some shopping."

"Here," Richard said, handing his sister the car keys. "I'm going to walk. I want to stop by the gallery. There's a marvellous painting I want to buy."

"Smashing," Magda replied. "Come on, Stellar. Let's go."

It was much more comfortable in the front seat of the car than the back. Magda turned on the radio, which blasted out a song as she tore into traffic, narrowly missing a scooter. It seemed like in their regard for the road, as with most things, brother and sister were very much alike.

"I think we'll just have a little squint at King's Road," Magda said as they zoomed up the street. "Or Carnaby Street. Yes. Let's start there. I just need a few things."

A pedestrian leapt out of the way as the Jaguar skimmed along, almost wiping off an entire row of wing mirrors. When they reached Carnaby Street, Magda didn't so much park the car as plunge it into a space that was much too small for it. Somehow, the laws of physics bent to Magda's will, and the car fit. Magda checked her pale pink lipstick as Estella regained her senses from the terrifying ride.

"All right!" Magda chirped. "Shopping!"

They had arrived at the very beating heart of Swinging London's shopping and fashion district. Estella observed Magda's gait as she led Estella down the road: she didn't bounce, precisely, but she lifted onto the balls of her feet and took long, elegant strides, emanating confidence and security with every step.

"So," Estella said, hustling to keep up, "Richard is writing a novel?"

"I doubt it," Magda said with a short laugh.

"But he said he was working on one?"

"I have no idea what he's on about. I just smile and nod. I don't think he knows, either, but that doesn't matter, does it? I'm sure he's quite brilliant. We have loads of brilliant people in our family. Now, we'll start here and work our way down..."

Out of the corner of her eye, Estella spotted a face across the street that she knew but could not immediately place. She turned to have a better look. It was a guy, and he had his arm around a girl with long black hair and the miniest white mini Estella had ever seen.

It was Michael, of the weird hair eating the night before. Magda looked over and saw the pair. "Is that Michael over there?" she asked.

Estella felt a sharp zip of nervousness come over her. What was she supposed to do? Steer Magda away? March across the street and punch him? She had absolutely no idea.

Magda nodded in greeting and smiled. Michael raised a hand in reply and continued walking, ogling the girl's endlessly long legs.

Estella looked between them, unable to make any sense of it.

Magda burst into laughter. "Your face!" she said.

"But... but he's your boyfriend!" Estella sputtered.

Magda looked genuinely confused. "I suppose, yes. What's the matter?"

"He's *your* boyfriend," Estella repeated.

"One mustn't be jealous or possessive," Magda stated as if it was obvious. "He can do as he likes and so can I. We're not ancient. No one gets hung up on things like that."

She said it in such a way that made Estella feel quite stupid. It was like Magda had just explained that the sun came up during the day.

"Oh," Estella said, stifling a cough. "Of course."

"Where *do* you come from?" Magda said. "It's so charming." She gave Estella a patronising smile. "There's so much to be *done* with you."

Estella might have resorted to blows had anyone else said that to her, in that way, but she had to admit Magda possibly had a point.

"That's Angie Walker-Weatherford he's with, anyway," Magda continued as they resumed walking. "She's loaded, different boy every minute, all that. So common. Always wears white – seems to think it's her signature, which is hilarious. She'd be pathetic except she knows the Ormsby-Gores and I think her sister is friends with Jane Asher from school." Magda patted her hair. "Cow," she said. "But if that's how he wants to spend his free time, that's his business. Now, let's have just the tiniest peep into Granny's..."

Estella made an agreeable noise with her throat, hoping that would be the end of it. She wasn't sure how to respond, swallowing her natural instinct to tell Magda she sounded petty and cruel. But what did Estella know of romantic relationships? It wasn't as though she'd ever had anything close to a boyfriend. Or any kind of close friend, really. Maybe that was just the way girls spoke about each other.

Estella shook off her discomfort and followed Magda into Granny Takes a Trip, the most illustrious, elite shop in all of London. Like at the Caterpillar, all the windows had been painted over, and the shopfront featured a pop art cartoon mural of a 1930s actress, all blonde hair and lips. Most shops used everything they could to entice buyers: signs, window dressings, the works. Granny Takes a Trip didn't seem even to want to be known as a shop.

This was one shop Estella had never even approached. It wasn't fear; there was nothing they could do to her. It was, perhaps, respect. After all, she entered most shops with the intention to steal. This shop was too cool for that, too impressive.

Inside, the shop was small, dark and hot. The wine-red walls and thick curtains didn't help much, nor did the racks of clothes – big furry coats, velvets, corduroys – that seemed to eat up all the space. Music was blasting, but not from the enormous antique gramophone that sat on a table. Weird old things were everywhere. It was madness.

Estella was in love. She drank it all in, growing almost woozy with delight. It seemed like Granny's actually made clothes out of the fabulous Liberty prints. And not just for women. There were magnificent jackets for men in the boldest patterns. At the back of the room was a man with a shock of curly hair and round tinted glasses. He casually rested against a cabinet as he advised people on their outfits.

"Hello, John," Magda called.

He nodded to Magda but kept his eyes on Estella.

"Where did you get that?" he asked, lowering his glasses on his nose as he looked at her dress.

"I made it," she said, lifting her chin.

"You made it?"

"That's what I just said."

He pushed his glasses back up and turned to Magda, as if waiting for an explanation.

"I found her," Magda said, examining a collection of scarves. "Isn't she marvellous?"

Someone like John wasn't about to admit that Estella was marvellous, but she could see him at least considering it.

They spent almost an hour at Granny's while Magda tried on clothes and twirled in front of John and Estella, who largely agreed on which outfits she should buy. The bottle-green skirt, yes. The black dress with the feather trim was not quite right. They disagreed on an electric-blue dress, but Estella won out, convincing Magda to leave it behind. Magda scooped up two more boas and a half dozen scarves, all in one breathless run of shopping that cost more than many people made in a week.

It would have been nothing at all for Estella to rob the place blind. There were no other staff, no floor walkers. The shop was so dark and cramped that she could have got an entire rack of clothes out without anyone being the wiser, even without any of her special gear. But she would not do that to Granny's, and she would never do it in front of Magda. It almost physically pained her not to quietly pinch one of the lovely scarves on the way out, but she held fast.

"Oh, John liked you!" Magda cooed when they emerged, blinking, into the sunlight. "Granny's is the absolute last word. I saw Anita in there once. She gets all her minis at Granny's."

"Anita?"

"Keith's girlfriend," Magda said, not quite rolling her eyes. "Oh, we really need to get you with it. Granny's was a good start. Now, come on. We need to get these things home."

8

THE MORESBY-PLUMS

THE DRIVE to Magda and Richard's house went across the city, all the way down to Chelsea, along the river. Estella found herself reaching religious fervour several times during the trip as they pushed a bus out of a lane, went through three red lights and twice mounted the pavement.

"Lovely car but dreadful steering!" Magda shouted over the music.

The little street Magda stopped the car on at last (and in one piece, thank goodness) was not just any little street. Cheyne Walk was right on the embankment, running along the Thames. It was a street with pedigree, with great wrought iron gates and ivy-covered walls. The cars parked along the curb were mostly Jaguars and Aston Martins, along with one massive white Rolls-Royce.

The pair exited the car, and Magda pushed open the gate of a townhouse dripping with purple wisteria from the ground to the third storey. The house continued for another storey above that.

"This is... your place?" she asked.

"Oh yaaaahs," Magda said. (She did say *yaaaahs*, not *yes* or *yeah*. It was a long, plummy word coming from her. Estella tried to feel the sound in her mouth to re-create later. *Yaaaaaahs*. She would work on it at home.)

"All of it?"

"Of course!" Magda laughed. "It's a nice place, really. Mick and Marianne live just there." She pointed a few paces away. "We see them quite often."

They entered a cool, dark foyer. In front of them was a staircase twisting up and around to the higher floors, with a stained glass window on the landing and paintings lining nearly every inch of the wall space. A massive grandfather clock stood straight ahead, in the crook between the stairs and the passage leading to the back of the house. Beside them was a massive marble, rosewood, mirror and brass structure – a kind of reception station for hats and packages. Magda dumped her bags there unceremoniously and slipped ahead, through some doors to the right, into the sitting room. This room was covered in dark panels, with two long and low crimson sofas facing each other over a marble-topped coffee table. Cushions filled the floor space.

"Bet-ty!" Magda called.

A woman, maybe about sixty years old, emerged from somewhere in the house. She wore a grey serving dress and a white apron.

"Yes, Miss Moresby-Plum?"

"It's so hot outside." Magda fanned herself for effect. "Bring us something cool? A sparkling lemonade?"

"Of course, miss."

Estella tried not to openly gape. Magda and Richard had servants. In their house. Or at least one servant, but any servant was bizarre and extraordinary.

"I'm so tired," Magda said, kicking off her little gold sandals. "I love the summer, but London is terrible in the heat. We thought about going away, but this summer promised to be so fun that we're just going to have to grin and bear it, even if it's beastly."

Betty had returned with a wooden tray containing two fizzy lemonades with ice. *Ice*. Estella, Horace and Jasper had a fridge they had purchased off the back of a lorry for a tenner. Electricity in the Lair was patchy at best, as they were siphoning it from other buildings, so usually either the fridge was not very cool, or else it was catching on fire.

Betty had taken the liberty of adding some glazed ginger biscuits and shortbreads on a plate. Estella quietly made plans for pocketing them without Magda's noticing.

"There's something I want to show you," Magda announced.

Estella was just reaching for her drink. She snatched it, gulped down about half the glass, and then followed Magda out of the room. Magda had started up the stairs, which creaked, but not in the way that the floor of the Lair creaked. In the Lair, the floor seemed to be saying, "At any moment, I plan on collapsing and sending you to your death." Here the creak had the quality of a soothing purr, a symphonious sound that proclaimed, "Welcome home, welcome home, how we love you, welcome home."

All along the stairs were pictures of people in various styles of historical dress. Estella picked out the eighteenth- and nineteenth-century outfits, period by period. All the people had the same general look about their faces, the same sharp features and fair hair that Magda and Richard shared.

"Are these portraits of your relatives?" Estella asked as they climbed.

"Darling," she said with a mischievous smile, "the Moresby-Plums go back ever so far. Somebody did something for Elizabeth I, and that was the start of it all. My uncle is the Chancellor of the Exchequer, I think. Something to do with money, anyway. Dear Uncle Phillip does something frightfully important for the Queen. Letters, or hounds, or maybe something with ships. This house has been in the family for ages, as you can tell."

She waved a hand at the faces staring out from the wall. "You see, when our parents died, our relatives sent us away to school, and we lived with our uncle for a time, and for a while in Switzerland. This place was closed up, mostly. But now that we're eighteen, it's all ours. It's a lovely house. It's going to be a smashing pad for parties. But first we have to decorate it. That's our job for this summer. It's going to be very groovy. Lots of places to hang out. I saw something lovely in a shop – stacks of these colourful mattresses, with just these gorgeous spreads on them. Everyone could be on the floor and..."

They had reached the fourth floor, which Estella was pretty certain was the top floor of the house.

"As you can see, it needs so much work," Magda said. "Mother and Father were dreadfully into antiques." Her tone was light, but when Estella glanced at her, she saw something new in Magda's eyes: a hint of sadness. Despite all their obvious differences, there was something intangible that bound the two together: loss. Maybe they were more alike than Estella had thought.

"Some are lovely and some are ghastly," Magda continued, the vulnerability Estella had detected just a moment before completely gone. "I've put them all up here. I think some of these things might be useful, but I've no idea how to start..."

She threw open a set of double doors, revealing a long room that took up the entire front of the house all the way to the windows that led to the street. The room was filled with objects, like a mad little shop. A massive table, loaded down with boxes and crates, stood in the middle of the space. Porcelains were lined up in neat rows along the edge. Under the table were more boxes, several busts and rolled carpets. All around was furniture – sofas, chairs, gateleg tables, plant stands, urns, small statues, lamps, clocks. There was just enough room to walk between the objects.

"You see what I mean," Magda said, rolling her eyes. "Nightmare. No idea what's in here, but surely some things worth keeping. You have such a good eye. Would you mind just having a little look?"

Estella did not mind. It was all she could do not to leap forward and start tearing the boxes open. She could see one was full of antique laces and velvets. Another seemed to have some satin in it. There might be clothes as well. What if there were vintage dresses or furs? Her brain spun out in visions of Worth gowns, Vionnet dresses, Patou knits, Chanel suits...

"Of course," Estella said, keeping her voice cool.

"Lovely. I'll leave you to it. I've just got to phone someone. You can just..." Magda waved at the thing-ness of it all. "I'll have Betty bring up your drink," she said as she skipped back towards the stairs.

Estella wound her way cautiously around the narrow path, peering into open boxes. There was a whole box of things made of silver. Sets of cutlery. Tea services. It would be nothing to pocket some of it. Not even pocket – she could fill a bag, lower it out the window to the garden and pick it up later. They might even thank her for getting rid of some of the uglier things.

No, Estella scolded herself. They were her friends now. They'd just met, really, but they'd taken her in, allowed her in the house. That was what friends were, right?

Estella shook her head. She could think about all that later. Now it was time to dig, to explore all these wondrous things she could feel and hold. On first inspection, there were no trunks full of clothes. There were fabrics, though – curtains, tablecloths, wall hangings. A set of long magnificent lace curtains grabbed her attention – definitely handmade. Probably Edwardian. She could make those into the most amazing pair of sleeves. What if she made it into a canopy for a bed? That would be incredible – the light filtering through.

Estella lost track of time, so preoccupied that she didn't notice she was no longer alone in the room until she heard a throat clear. She looked up, expecting to see Betty and the fizzy lemonade.

It was not Betty.

"Hello," said a vaguely familiar male voice.

She looked up and saw Peter standing in the doorway. In full daylight, he was all the more striking, leaning against the door frame with a half-moon smile. He was wearing another fairly dull outfit – more brown trousers, this time paired with a floral shirt someone with pedestrian taste had probably told him was very 'with it'.

"Oh," she said. "Yes."

That was not how you answered "hello", and she was immediately filled with regret. He cocked his head curiously. "Are you dressed as a tin of beans?"

She was unsure from his tone what he made of her dress, but no matter. Confidence. She needed to exude it.

"No," she replied.

"No?"

"No. I am dressed as *many* tins of beans."

That got a big smile. He peeled himself away from the door and stepped into the room, regarding the piles of antiques.

"Looks like a jumble sale at the palace up here," he remarked. "Do you live here, too?"

"Me?" she said. "Here?"

He smiled. "That was the question, yeah."

"No," she replied. "No. I'm... I've never been here before. I'm helping. Magda asked me to look through these things."

"How about that?" He raised an eyebrow. "I've never been here before, either. Magda phoned me up, said she had some old instruments I might want a look at. And here I am, and here you are. It's a funny old world."

Estella realised she was gripping the curtains like they were a lifesaving rope. She commanded herself to relax, but it did not work. Her grip only tightened.

"There's some kind of instrument over there," she said, nodding to a piano-like object in the corner.

"Is there, now? Let's see what we've got here..." He loped over to the thing with a long, easy gait and pulled back the blanket that half covered it, revealing an ornate instrument with two keyboards. "Blimey."

"What is that?" Estella asked.

"A harpsichord," he replied.

He tried a few of the keys, and a foul tinny sound came out.

"A broken harpsichord," Peter amended. He tested more keys, which sounded progressively worse. Some made no sound at all.

"This might be beyond repair," he said. "Shame. Would have loved a harpsichord. See anything else?"

"I think there was something with strings over there," she said, pointing across the room.

He walked in the direction she'd indicated and picked up a rectangular wooden box with strings stretched across it.

"Now, what are you?" he murmured, turning it over in his hands and examining it. "You look like a lute, but you're too square. Nine strings as well. Very odd. Let's see what you sound like."

Peter worked his fingers along the neck of the instrument for a moment and plucked the strings. The noise seemed fine to Estella, but the result appeared to dissatisfy him. He frowned, fiddled with the tuning and tried again. This time, the plinking had a cleaner, rounder tone.

"How did you do that?" Estella said. "I thought you didn't know what that is."

He shrugged. "I don't. I just guessed. Lots of instruments are alike."

"How many instruments do you play?" Estella asked.

"I don't know," he said, plucking away.

"How could you not know how many instruments you play?"

"Because I don't really think about it that way," he replied. "I just play with them when I find them, and I seem to make some music come out of them. I never was much good at learning anything else, but I can play most instruments I try. Like this."

Carefully, with his fingertips, he found a little song.

"That's like me with fabric," Estella said. "I just know what to do with it."

He stopped playing and regarded her for a long moment.

"So do you think it's a coincidence that you've never been here before and I've never been here before, and we've both been invited over on the same day?" he asked.

"Possibly not," Estella said.

Peter smiled. "No. I think they might be up to something."

Estella realised she was holding her breath tight and low in her belly, like it was a bomb that might go off if she let up on the pressure. Peter played a few more notes on the strange little box instrument. *Plink, plink, plink.*

She had no idea what should happen next. *Say something. Anything. Just move the moment on.*

"I was looking at your album last night," Estella ventured.

"Well, that's where you've made your mistake. You're supposed to listen to it."

"I was looking," she said again, "at the back. At the song names. Your name is listed after all of them. And your name was by a lot of the instruments, as well. If you do all the writing and play all of the instruments, why is Chris the famous one?"

"Because I'm just the guitarist. The singer's what matters."

"Why?"

"'Cause he's out front," he reasoned.

"That doesn't seem fair."

"Never said things had to be fair."

"Don't you want to be noticed?"

"I want to be listened to," Peter said. "But I'm not sure about noticed."

That didn't entirely make sense to Estella. If she had the opportunity, she would choose to be noticed all the time. The only time she tried to avoid it was when she was lifting things from shops or unsuspecting pockets.

"We're going to be on telly in a few weeks' time," he said. "I suppose we'll be noticed then."

"Really! What are you going to wear?"

"Wear?" he repeated, as though it was a foreign word. "No idea. We all share a flat, and we have a pile of clothes we take from – except for Chris. He has his own. I just pick up whatever's on the floor closest to me and wear that. We're all about the same size."

Estella nearly wanted to clap her hands over her ears at hearing all that. "No, no," she said, shaking her head. "You can't do that. You need something of your own. Something special."

"Like what?"

"I could... make you something," she said. "Something

incredible. You would stand out. People wouldn't be able to stop looking at you."

"Is that a good thing?" he asked.

"Of course."

Peter leaned back and smiled.

"How about this," he said. "You make me something to wear, and I'll write you a song."

Estella blushed, then nodded. She would make something fit for a rock star, and her design would be the talk of everyone who saw it. *Her* design.

"I need paper. I need to draw."

"Here." He opened his bag and pulled out a notebook and pencil. "I always carry some for writing songs."

"Stand like you would when you play guitar," she instructed.

"You want me to pose?"

Estella nodded. "The clothes have to move with you."

Peter shifted a bit, then stood with one hip slightly cocked to the right. He lifted the weird little box instrument and held it like a guitar.

"This is too small," he said. "But normally I'd have one hand up here" – he indicated where he held the neck of the instrument – "and another here." He nodded towards his hip. Estella circled Peter, taking in his shape, his size. She did a rough sketch, becoming less self-conscious of how she reacted to Peter's presence with every pencil mark. Once Estella started drawing, she often went into a state in which she didn't see or notice anything but the colours and shapes that filled her head. She would need some preliminary measurements, but it was unlikely Magda and Richard had anything as pedestrian and practical as a tape measure. She dug around in the boxes until she found something useful in the form of heavy pull cord.

"Are you making an outfit or a sofa?" Peter asked, still in his pose.

"I'll make a mark on it," she explained. "Use it as a measure."

She held the cord against his arm, from his shoulder to his wrist. His skin was warm. She had measured and fitted Jasper and Horace many times, but she had never felt like this doing it. She felt Peter's pulse beating down into his hand.

"Never had bespoke before," he said, looking down at her. She could feel his breath on the side of her face.

"Turn," she said, her voice coming out hoarser than she would have liked. "Have to do your back."

She held the cord to the points of his shoulders, then from the nape of his neck to the small of his back. Her thoughts were getting fuzzy, and she had to continually refocus.

"I just need an outside measurement," she said, bending down to stretch the cord from his hip to his ankle.

The whole process took only a minute or two, but it felt like a day, a month, maybe even a year had gone by. The plastic of Estella's dress squeaked in protest as she stood up.

"Have to be going," he said after they were both silent for a moment. "Rehearsal. But I suppose we'll be seeing each other again."

"I suppose so," she said.

"My telephone number." He wrote the number down on the edge of a page from his notebook. "For when it's time to make our trade."

He placed it into Estella's palm. She closed her fingers around it.

"I'll take this thing, whatever it is," he said, tucking the strange box instrument under his arm. "Let me know when to pick up my new clothes."

He walked to the door, plinking the new instrument as he went.

"I like beans a lot, by the way," Peter said over his shoulder when he had reached the door. "They're my favourite."

9

UNFAMILIAR FEELINGS

WHEN ESTELLA descended the stairs once Peter had left, she felt a light buzzing sensation in her head and stopped for a moment to look out the stained glass panel on the first floor landing and compose herself. Magda was waiting for her, sprawled out on a carpet on the sitting room floor, looking through a magazine. She rolled over as Estella continued down the stairs.

"Well?" she said, smiling. "Did Peter find anything he liked?"

Estella went into the room and sat on the edge of the sofa.

"You did that on purpose," she said.

"Well, of course. I was a *bit* naughty. How did it go?"

Estella had no idea how it had gone, and she knew her expression indicated as much. Magda rolled back and forth on the floor and laughed her tinkling little laugh.

"It's not funny," Estella said.

Magda stopped rolling and propped herself up on one bent elbow.

"It's perfectly hilarious. You seemed to get on at the party, so I wanted to speed things up a bit. You two would make a good pair. He likes you."

"No, he doesn't," Estella said, rolling her eyes.

"Of course he does! When I rang him and said you were here, he dropped whatever nonsense he was up to and came right over. Just what you need for this summer, a nice pop star for your arm. They're all the rage. Drop whatever boyfriend you've got now and take this one."

"I... I don't... I never... have."

Magda froze, her eyes wide in interest.

"You never have what?"

Estella's cheeks grew hot with embarrassment. She

wanted to crawl out of her skin. Just unzip it, drop it, ooze away between the floorboards.

"Haven't you *had* a boyfriend before?" Magda asked, a little smile twisting on her lips. "Can thieves not have boyfriends?"

"It's never come up," Estella said. "And I'm a not thief, remember? I'm a designer. Who steals."

"Well, this is perfect!" Magda said. "You're two artists, and you should have some fun together." She clapped her hands in delight. "Oh, you're the very best project I've ever had."

Estella had no idea what to say. No one had ever spoken to her like that.

"It's all right," Magda said, her voice taking on a softer tone. "I'll walk you through it. This is what friends do, you know. And I quite enjoy a challenge."

Friends? Was that what they were? Real, actual girlfriends? And a boyfriend? All this... all this life that hadn't even been an option the previous day was now laid out in front of her like a strange, grand feast. Friends with people who lived in houses like this? Designing clothes and dating pop stars?

The image of the couple entwined with each other on the grass in the park came back into her mind.

Maybe she could have that. She could have all of it.

"You need to start coming round every day," Magda proclaimed. "It's going to be a fun summer. You wait and see."

All sorts of soft, unfamiliar feelings bubbled up inside her as she walked towards the bus stop later that afternoon. It was like she was seeing London for the very first time. How had she never noticed how obviously wonderful the city was? All the rich smells – the fish and chips, the ale from the pubs, the sweet grass in the park and the flowering trees. Everyone's face was kind, and she had warm feelings for everyone she passed. She wanted all of it; she wanted to drink it up and never stop.

Magda. Friend.

The more she thought it over, the more Estella realised she'd never had any friends. There had been one girl at school who was nice enough to her. And when she came to London, she'd found Jasper and Horace, but they were something more than friends – family, more like, albeit an odd one.

And then there was Peter. Boyfriend? Just thinking of his name made her want to laugh. Peter, with his heart-shaped face and his slow smile. She would help him become what he was meant to be. She could see it now – the clothes, a bit of a haircut. She could give him the tools he needed to be everything he clearly already was and more. A star.

And in turn, designing for Peter would help Estella become recognised in her own way, among her own sort of people. Two dreamers, two artists, turned famous for the mastery of their respective crafts. Drawn together by passion. She could see it all.

It's not real, whispered Cruella. *It can't be. Friends, romance – these things are for other people. Not you.*

Estella understood why Cruella would be a bit suspicious. What did friends want from you? Like Horace had asked: what was the angle? The existence they led didn't exactly lend itself to trusting people. And Cruella definitely didn't get crushes.

But that night, Estella wanted to be Estella, and Estella only.

"Thank you for coming," Estella replied, "but you may go now."

Listen to me. You think you can have this? You live in a hovel. You have nothing.

"You may go now," Estella repeated.

He's going to find out what you really are, and then where will you be?

"Goodbye, Cruella," Estella said.

"I need to do a run today," Estella said the next morning as the boys woke and ambled to the kitchen for some breakfast. "For fabric. One of you has to be my eyes."

After returning to the Lair the previous night, Estella had stayed up nearly until dawn, too wound up to sleep, instead plotting out the details of Peter's new clothes. She'd pored over every borrowed book she had on court dress before narrowing her focus to the eighteenth-century tome that was her favourite. She would start with something a French courtier might have worn to call on Marie Antoinette. It would begin with a coat that would fall just below the hip, with large turned cuffs and a high-standing collar. She first considered embroidering the entire thing, but that would take her all summer. Perhaps just some crewelwork – that ancient embroidery technique oft used on tapestries – on the cuffs of Peter's jacket. Funny, wasn't it, that the word *cruel* came up in sewing?

Finally, she decided she would take small bits of fabric and sew together an elaborate design like she had with her dress. Running down the right arm would be streams of brown silk coming from a teapot on the upper back. On the lower back, a teacup. She would use orange, blue and yellow silk to sew lightning bolts coming out of it. Estella would bring the Electric Teacup to life on the jacket.

She could make matching trousers, as well, continuing the lightning bolt theme. There would be a shirt, too. Lots of the guys on Carnaby Street had been wearing shirts with elaborate flowing bits in the front. She would make his of lace, which she would hand-embellish with gold thread. It would be magnificent. No one would have anything like it. But first she would need the base material. Something of exceptional quality, and lots of it. That, of course, meant going back to Liberty.

Jasper took one of the blank tins of beans from the pile, opened it, and dumped it into a saucepan.

"What are we doing?" he asked.

Estella walked to the rack of disguises and surveyed them, her brow furrowed in concentration. "Think it has to be Edna and Fred," she said.

Jasper whistled through his teeth. "Getting out the big guns," he said. "I'll find some mice once I've eaten."

Edna and Fred were reserved for special cases in which Estella's standard hidden pockets and false-bottom items simply wouldn't do. The result was a conventional, bookish pair whose success relied on two things: giant underpants and mice. The giant underpants weren't knickers; they were bloomer-like things, with tight elastic around the ankles. They required larger clothes to effectively obscure them. When they were used correctly, one could perform frankly astonishing feats of petty thievery. Estella had stolen multiple coats (furs squashed down nicely, though they were quite warm), a kettle, loads of groceries, even a handful of small rugs. Once she'd even got a mirror in there – not full length, of course, but big enough.

Estella began to dress, pulling herself into the giant

underpants and then the long skirt that covered them. Jasper and Horace were making their way around the Lair, looking for mice, the greatest and most useful of natural resources.

"All right," Jasper said, getting into Fred's fussy tweed suit and filling the inside pockets of his trousers with tiny furry friends. "Let's go."

"Make it snappy," Jasper said under his breath as they exited the lift on Liberty's fabric floor. "I feel a revolution brewing in the trouser department."

Estella glanced sidelong at her partner and saw that the mice were visibly wriggling around. She had a good idea of what she wanted, and she quickly settled on an indigo velvet that had a silvery sheen.

"Now," she said to Jasper.

Jasper walked to the far end of the fabric floor and pulled on a cord in his pocket, which opened a different, tearaway pocket further down, near his ankle. The mice spilled out over his shoe. He walked away, letting the mice do their work.

It took only a moment for one of the shop assistants to look down and see the trail of disgruntled mice running across the floor. When the scream came, Estella knocked the roll of fabric to the floor and knelt by it. Jasper held the roll as she began unspooling the fabric, feeding it down into the waistband of the giant bloomers, stuffing as she went. Down, down, down. Pounds and pounds of velvet. Her skirt ballooned out. He helped her to her feet. The masses of fabric made walking difficult; her feet pointed out to the sides.

"How horrible!" she said as they left the way they came. "Mice! In Liberty!"

Moments later, they were back out on the street, Estella waddling along in her velvet-filled bloomers.

"Did we have to do Edna and Fred on a day like this?" Jasper grumbled, loosening his collar.

"What are you complaining about? I'm the one with a hundred pounds' worth of velvet in her bloomers."

"Well, *I've* got a dozen mouse bites on my leg," Jasper sniped.

At the first possible opportunity, Estella ducked into an alley to remove the fabric from under her skirt.

"Here," she said, thrusting the velvet at Jasper. "You take it for a while. I need to walk with my legs pointing in the same direction for a moment."

As they continued towards the bus stop, Estella thought of how nice it would be in the future when her fabric was delivered to her. She would be sitting in her eponymous atelier, sipping a glass of wine, looking over her table of designs when it arrived – loads of it, more than she could ever use. Estella let herself sink into the familiar fantasy, where it was always approaching dusk, with the lights of London twinkling outside. She had a room of dummies wearing her in-progress creations. There were furs in this fantasy, too. Lots of furs. Wonderful trims, exquisite collars, resplendent coats. Her atelier was cool and perfectly lit. It smelled of jasmine perfume. And in the background, the musical sound of sewing machines—

"Really good mouse haul today, as well," Jasper commented, jarring Estella out of her reverie, as he hefted the bundle onto the bus. "I don't think it's ever been so easy to get so many of them. Must be the weather."

Estella grunted a reply. There were no mice in her fantasy atelier. Mice were banned.

Estella spent the next few days drawing, tossing aside and redrawing.

The sleeves were too wide.

Taper them a bit.

When Peter moved his arm with the guitar, the cuff would strike the strings.

Take off the buttons.

Sew the cuffs down.

She was working over the design for what had to have been the twentieth time when Jasper leaned over her worktable and tapped his finger on the surface to get her attention.

"Is anyone at home?" he asked.

She looked up from her sketches. A bead of sweat rolled down her nose and landed on the pad.

"Come on, Stel," he said. "We've done nothing in two days."

"I've been working," she said, blinking. Her eyes had to refocus on a human face. She had been very close to her sketchpad.

"What's that for? What kind of disguise is that?"

"It's not," she said, snapping her drawing pad shut. "It's one of my personal designs."

"Well, we need to get to work."

"Yeah," Horace chimed in. "Every day we're not out there is wasted. It's all tourists! It's good pickings out there."

"Come on," Jasper said, playfully bopping her on the shoulder. "Come out in the sunshine, Stel. Let's go have a little fun."

It was true that it was a blazing sunny day. It would be perfect for a little outing.

"All right," she agreed. "We'll do a run."

"Now we're talking," Jasper said with a smile. "Whatcha fancy? Grab some wallets along Piccadilly?"

Estella looked down at the pile of newspapers she kept on the floor by her sewing table. Something caught her eye, a perfect way to get in an afternoon of heisting and fashion education at the same time. She picked it up.

"What if we set our sights a bit higher?" she asked, spreading out the paper on the ground and pointing to an article that read EXHIBITION OF YOUTH FASHION TO BE HELD AT SAVOY HOTEL.

"This," she said, tapping on the article. "We go to this."

"To a fashion show?"

"At the Savoy."

"The Savoy," Jasper repeated.

"What?" Horace said. "That posh hotel?"

"The poshest," Estella replied.

"Why would we go to a fashion show?" Jasper asked.

"Because," she said, "the people who go to them are very rich, and they pay no attention to their stuff. They're careless." This was a central principle of the rich the trio had always assumed – that they were careless with their possessions, and that such carelessness translated directly into the group's pockets. Since having forged her new friendships, Estella now knew it to be true.

"Dunno," Horace said. "We could do just as well at a cheaper place and there's no lookout on those. Lots of tourists. Easy pickings."

"But think of what we could get at the Savoy," Estella said. "One wallet there is worth five or six somewhere else."

Horace considered that for a moment.

"Could do the dodgy-tummy run, I suppose," he finally said. "Stel goes in, does the deed, leaves the drop for us."

The dodgy-tummy run was pretty much what it sounded like: one of the party would go to an event, swiping wallets and trinkets and watches along the way, stuffing them into false pockets. They would then grasp their middle, holding the takings under their arms, and run to the toilets. No one asked questions if you grasped your middle and ran to the toilets. No one wanted to know. Once there, the wallets and other goods would be removed and tossed into the bin in the toilets. Another member of the party would come and remove the trash. And that was that. Simple and very effective. It worked pretty much every time.

"That means I have to be Mrs Hooverbottom, doesn't it?" Jasper groaned. "First Fred, now her, but all right. As long as we do a job."

"We could still do the park," Horace said. "Safer, easier."

"What's the point in that?" Estella asked, trying not to show her frustration.

"Not getting caught."

Estella smiled. "Well, that doesn't sound like much fun."

"I don't like it when you smile like that," Horace said.

10

KNIT IT TOGETHER

THE SOLES of Estella's shoes made a neat clicking sound on the black-and-white tiled floor of the Savoy lobby. While the rest of London swelled in the heat, it was cool and dark inside the Savoy; not even the elements could infringe on the comfort of its guests. Like Harrods, the Savoy was one of those London institutions that seemed to be willing to go to any lengths to serve and satisfy. For instance, an Indian prince who had stayed there recently had left something of import to him at home. Instead of having it sent via regular mail or a delivery service, the Savoy had sent a messenger to India to retrieve it.

Even during the war, the Savoy had prided itself on maintaining perfect service as the bombs fell all around and the city shook. Sometimes the guests had been forced to sleep in the lobby for safety, but they did so in relative comfort while being exquisitely attended to by the staff.

Tradition.

Order.

Service.

No Swinging London here. If there were to be fashion shows held on the premises, and of course there were, they would be done in Savoy style as the very best of London's society – 'best' meaning the people who had been richest the longest and had the most last names – surveyed the goods on offer.

Estella needed to look reasonably with-it while still appearing serious enough to be going to the Savoy to write about an exhibition of youth fashion. A plain white dress. (Mini, but not too mini. It was really almost a knee-length.) Knee socks. A long blonde wig. The ensemble was completed by a satchel, one of Estella's many modified bags with a hidden lining. Around her neck was a camera, one the trio had lifted from a tourist the past summer. There was no film inside.

Horace would be taking the role of messenger, a glorified errand boy ostensibly waiting in the lobby to do the bidding of one of the Savoy's guests. He would be the lookout, making sure Estella got in and out safely, and signalling Jasper to go in to do the cleaning and empty the bin.

Jasper, or Mrs Hooverbottom, had gone ahead. He was sitting on one of the overstuffed sofas in the lobby, pretending to do the *Sunday Times* crossword puzzle. He lifted his glance only for a moment, to acknowledge Estella's arrival. Horace would soon follow.

There was a sign on an easel indicating which ballroom the show was being held in. Estella sneaked covert glances at the other girls and women who were headed inside, noting that the overwhelming majority didn't seem like the sort who rode the bleeding edge of youth fashion. There were some younger-looking women, maybe in their late teens or early twenties, mostly dressed similarly to Estella: conservative skirts, simple blouses, exceedingly dull dresses, pearls and a few brooches that were truly criminal in their ugliness. Many of the young women had their mothers or aunts with them, the older generation clad in Chanel-type suits, white gloves and pillbox or feathered hats. Those without hats had their hair formally styled into teased helmet shapes. The smell of eau de cologne in the queue was strong enough to peel the silk wallpaper from the walls.

"I'm here for the exhibition of youth fashion," Estella said to the man standing at the door once she'd made her way to the front of the queue. She used her plummiest accent and lifted her camera as proof.

"Your invitation, please?"

Estella reached into her pocket. She had no invitation, of course, but the idea was to make a show of looking there, then in her bag, and then to appear increasingly distressed.

"I'm here to write about the show for *Teen Pulse*. I—I have one, it's here somewhere..." she stammered.

The man at the door waited patiently.

"It's my first time out of the office on assignment," she squeaked, letting a little tremble come into her voice. "Oh, I'll be sacked! Sacked! We need the photographs!"

The man softened. This wasn't a royal luncheon, after all. "All right," he said quietly, giving her an encouraging smile. "Go ahead."

"Oh," Estella said, gasping, "thank you! Thank you! My mum thanks you, too!"

She hurried in before he could say another word.

A low stage had been set up along one of the ballroom walls, a pop art backdrop installed behind it, great big circles in black and white and orange dotted with signs printed in bold letters that said things like FASHION NOW, YOUTHQUAKE, FREEDOM and KNIT IT TOGETHER.

"That doesn't even make sense," Estella mumbled under her breath. "Knit what together?"

London's finest waiting staff glided as if on skates between the tables situated around the stage, distributing tiered china plates of cucumber, egg and crab salad finger sandwiches. They poured tea from silver pots. More staff appeared with serving trays of sweet treats – Battenberg slices, scones, meringues, lemon biscuits and cream buns. The room was filled with the gentle music of spoons tinkling inside teacups and a murmur of subdued conversation. The garish decorations of the stage clashed with the posh, muted mood of the room in every way.

It was a profoundly depressing scene. They dared call it a fashion event?

Estella took up a position in the corner of the room, near the edge of the stage. From there, she could survey the tops of the tables quite easily. The photographer bit was a particularly good one: getting on the floor, kneeling down right next to people, pointing the camera up with both hands, then promptly lowering the camera and letting it hang from its strap as you pretended to adjust something or reach for more film. From there, it was nothing at all to slip your hand into the various open bags sitting by people's feet or hung across the backs of their chairs.

Some jazzy music began to play over the speakers, and the lights dimmed.

"Ladies!" boomed a voice. "Welcome to this afternoon's exhibition of youth fashion, featuring the finest names in today's design!"

Estella heard her jaw click as she shifted it.

Some swirly lights came on and a series of models came out. They walked slowly, doing a strange bouncy-kneed dance while showing off some tragically uninspired matching sweater-and-skirt sets.

"The most exciting trends in knitwear!" the announcer continued. "Can you dig it, ladies?"

"Oh god," Estella said to herself.

That was the thing about fashion now in London that the old guard seemed perpetually to misunderstand: it wasn't coming from above, from the big houses. It came from people like her, from the mood on the street and in the clubs. What she was seeing here was a mere pale imitation. The colours, while garish, were all wrong. It was worse when the models sauntered past clad in pieces that were *almost* right – a decent pair of boots that narrowly missed the mark of fashion-forward or a just-to-the-left-of-acceptable hat. It was like listening to someone play music and get every fifth note wrong, constantly jangling. Estella felt a huge boost of confidence as she saw creation after creation parade down the runway and knew she could do better than every single one of them – in her sleep.

All the well-heeled young women and their mothers in their elaborate hats mumbled in low, polite tones and made notes on the little pads of paper they'd been given, marking down which of the terrible knitwear sets they were going to order.

It was a genuine kindness to those clothes that Estella had no film to record them. Let them die and be forgotten.

Estella turned and saw a nearby handbag, fat with visible cash, open by a woman's leather pump.

Time to work.

She knelt with her camera, fishing in the handbag with one hand as she pretended to snap photos with the other. Another handbag dangled from the back of a chair – low-hanging fruit. Around she went, kneeling and picking. It was almost too easy. Her bag was filling fast.

As she was about to leave the room, Estella noticed a particularly posh silver cigarette case sitting out in plain view. It was too lovely not to take. She reached over, slipped it gently off the table and continued towards the door.

Just then, a model wearing a particularly horrific outfit bounded onto the stage. It was enough to make Estella freeze in her tracks. It was so hard to comprehend what they had done. It was a clingy mustard-yellow skirt-and-sweater set, trimmed in powder blue and violent pink, as though the designer had endeavoured to combine every single precise shade that would offend the human eye into a single outfit. It needed to be shot into space.

"What are you doing with my cigarette case?" someone said.

Estella jolted back into the moment, realising she had been so distracted by the fashion crime onstage that she'd forgotten about her own petty crime taking place in the audience and had neglected to put the case in her bag. The case's owner – a middle-aged woman in a purple Chanel suit, looking not unlike a giant grape – was staring at her accusingly.

"Oh, erm..." Estella felt a rush of panic. *Get it together.* "Oh, I'm sorry. I thought..."

"You thought what?" the woman asked hotly.

Good question.

"I thought it was... mine?" Estella's statement came out more like a query, and seemed to do very little to assuage the angry purple woman.

By then the exchange was attracting attention from nearby tables. The models were still bobbing away along the catwalk, and the people close to them were mostly watching the show. But Estella saw the ripple of awareness go through the room. People liked to know when something was going on, and in this case, many of those people were about to realise that their own purses were missing. That meant she had to leave, now, quietly and quickly and without fuss.

"I don't feel well," Estella said, lowering her voice and putting one hand to her head. "I'm dizzy. I'm so sorry. I need to find the toilets."

Estella replaced the case on the table and walked determinedly out of the room. Behind her, she heard conversations and, very faintly, someone talking about a purse. She moved a bit faster. No one did anything to stop her, because no one knew what to make of what was going on. Confusion was a thief's best friend. By the time people worked out what had happened, you were already gone.

She'd made it through the doorway and back into the lobby when she heard the voice of the man by the door, the one who had let her in without an invitation.

"You," he called out.

When one was stealing and heard the word *you*, the impulse was to run.

That was not always the best course of action.

In fact, it was almost always better to slow down. Pretend it wasn't you who had been told to stop. Also, fancy places like the Savoy didn't want chase scenes being enacted in their lobbies. The whole point of the Savoy was that it was quiet, calm and proper, and something as common as thieving did not happen there.

The man caught up to Estella and stood in front of her.

"I need to speak with you," he said.

"I'm not well," she said weakly, holding her bag harder. "Toilets, please. Please. Which way?" She'd worked up a sweat on the move, her glistening skin adding to the impression that she was ill.

Again, confusion. Some might say the Savoy's distaste for thievery could be matched by its repugnance for girls vomiting in its lobby.

"Follow me," the man said sternly.

Out of the corner of her eye, Estella saw Horace waiting with an empty box that had been made up to look like a parcel he needed to deliver. She gently inclined her head in an attempt to convey that she was all right. If she could get to the toilets, she could unload everything she had on her.

But the man guided her in a different direction.

"This way," he said. "We have private ones if you are not well."

"Oh," she said, putting a hand to her mouth. "Oh. Oh, no..."

She staggered a few steps forward, towards where she

knew the public toilets were located. The man reached out to assist her. He would help her get there; she would be able to pull this off. She saw Jasper, in his wig and dress, hovering, waiting to follow her in.

And then Estella tripped.

It happened, especially if you were walking hunched over, clutching a bag full of smaller handbags and assorted valuables, trying to stumble your way along. And it would not have mattered except that the man reached out to steady her, and instead of grasping her shoulder, he accidentally latched on to her wig, finding himself holding a long swath of blonde hair in one hand.

At that point, Estella decided that running was the best course of action.

She broke for the door. But security was already closing in. She wasn't going to make it.

"There goes another one!" Jasper yelled in his Mrs Hooverbottom voice.

Some of the staff turned in his direction and saw an elderly woman with a large knitting bag, who, on closer inspection, might not be as she appeared. He took off running in the opposite direction, deeper into the hotel. Horace opted to follow Jasper, making a split-second decision as to where his presence would most come in handy. The chaos gave Estella just enough clearance to squeeze through the gauntlet by the door and make it outside.

Their rendezvous point in case of emergency was the Victoria Gardens Park by the Victoria Embankment, just a short run from the Savoy but far enough to allow them to bleed back into the city. She ran directly into the public toilet there, where she locked herself into a stall, pulled off her dress, and turned it inside out. The dress went from a placid white to an eye-catching blue and red. She pulled a thin red scarf from the bottom of her bag and quickly wound it around her head, then added a pair of sunglasses. Estella dug into the bag and found that she had managed to steal over two hundred pounds, which was enough to keep them afloat for most of the summer. She had also obtained from the purses in the ballroom several credit cards, a small bottle of lily of the valley perfume, two lipsticks, a very attractive compact mirror and a silver lighter.

Estella dumped the stolen wallets behind the cistern after removing their contents, stepped out of the stall and put on a coat of white lipstick. She pulled off her shoes and traipsed barefoot out onto the grass, where she collapsed into a seated position on the ground.

It was another ten minutes before Horace jogged up, red-faced and out of breath. He dropped down next to her.

"Too close," Horace gasped, leaning over to catch his breath. "Told you we shouldn'ta gone there. Shoulda… shoulda stuck with the park. Jasper…"

"Where is he?"

"Went up in the lift. I tried to follow him but they started looking at me funny, so I got out."

Estella bit down on her lip. Jasper could very well be wandering the halls of the Savoy, shedding bits of his disguise as he went. Like Estella's dress, Mrs Hooverbottom's clothes had hidden aspects, such as trousers that were rolled up to the knee and secured to the inside of the dress so the skirt could be detached and pulled off as needed. He wore a men's shirt under the ladies' wool jacket. He had his regular shoes in his massive knitting bag.

"What do you think we should do?" Horace asked.

"We wait for him," she replied. "If we don't see him soon, we start checking the local nicks."

A full hour later, Jasper, no longer dressed as Mrs Hooverbottom, arrived at the gardens.

"We thought they got you," Horace cried.

"They did get me," Jasper replied. "But there's no crime in hanging about the Savoy in a disguise. I said it was part of a student prank. They didn't believe me, but they had nothing on me, so they just chucked me out, told me not to come back."

"Too close," Horace said again.

"But we made it," Estella protested. "And we got away with all this stuff!" She motioned to her bag, which was bursting with goodies. "Over two hundred pounds! Two *hundred*!"

That was a lot. A fortune. But Horace just shook his head. "Too close," he replied, sounding disgruntled. "Should have kept it simple. Should have gone to the park. Could have got what we needed, had an ice cream, no problems."

"Horace has a point," Jasper agreed.

"Course I have a bleeding point!"

"Where's your sense of adventure?" Estella asked. "Come on. You loved it."

Neither Jasper nor Horace looked like he had loved it, but Estella would not be dismissed. They didn't get it. This summer, things were happening. Her clothes. Her life. It was all coming together. Sometimes, to get things you wanted, you needed to be bold. You needed to step out and take risks, to deviate from your normal pattern.

In that moment, she caught sight of a painful corollary: if she followed Jasper and Horace and continued to play by their rules, her life would stay the same forever.

11

THE MAGIC BEAN GIRL

AFTER THE near miss at the Savoy, the trio decided to lie low for a little while. Estella figured it was for the best; there was some leftover tension in the group over who had been at fault for the dust-up (Jasper and Horace blamed her, whereas Estella took a more cosmic view) and whether the reward had been worth the risk. She thought they could all benefit from a short cooling-off period.

Jasper and Horace had no desire to spend the long summer days in the stuffy Lair, and they ventured out with their comic books to linger in the park. Estella often spent the afternoons with Magda and Richard, meeting them at the Caterpillar and going back to their house to lounge. She now had a standing invitation and no longer needed to knock. When you were in, you were in, and if the door was unlocked, you were welcome inside. That was how the London scene worked – people drifting in and out of each other's rooms and orbits.

The rest of her time was spent on Peter's outfit. The Electric Teacup's television appearance was coming up soon. Estella worked morning and night at her sewing table whenever she wasn't out with her new friends. Buddy and Wink kept her company. Piece by piece, the ensemble came together. She pinned, stitched, dressed the mannequin, scrutinised every element. The shell of the jacket was there, along with some of the initial detail work for the pattern. She would need to fit Peter properly before she could finish it.

That meant phoning him. For some reason, that prospect was daunting. They had no telephone at the Lair, which had never mattered, since Estella never had anyone to call. She was unsure how to address Peter, having not seen him since their moment in Magda's house. Should she be professional, as though she were calling from a shop? Should she be friendly, like at a party? Should she be flirtatious? Did she even know how to be flirtatious?

Annoyed with herself for overthinking what should have been a simple phone call, Estella finally marched herself down to the phone box on the corner, closed herself inside and squeezed the coin before she put it in the slot and dialled the number Peter had given her. It rang five times.

"Hello?" someone shouted. The voice was loud and staticky over the pulsing sound of music in the background.

"Peter?" Estella yelled back. "Is this Peter?"

"Peter?"

"Peter!"

"Wait, wait, wait... turn it down a bit, mate! Turn it down a bit!"

No one turned it down a bit.

"Peter?" the person repeated.

"Peter," Estella replied, sighing and leaning against the wall of the phone box.

"Oh. Wait. I'll get him."

She heard the receiver being clunked down. There

was conversation; then the music turned way down in the background.

"Hello?"

A warm feeling spread through her on hearing Peter's voice. "Hi, Peter. It's Estella."

"Estella! Almost done my suit?"

"Almost done my song?" she replied, smiling.

"I don't know if the Greek muses were so demanding. We need to get a better class of muse these days, I tell you."

Estella laughed. "I need to make sure it fits before I do the detailing," she said. "You need to try it on so I can finish it."

"You're in luck," he replied. "I'm free. Where's your flat?"

"Oh..." She had been intending to tell him to meet her at Magda and Richard's. It had never even occurred to her that he would want to come to the Lair. "I was thinking Cheyne Walk?"

"Isn't it easier if I come to you? You do live in London, don't you?"

"I... do."

"Okay. So where's your flat?"

"My flat isn't... very nice," Estella said, feeling her cheeks flush.

Peter laughed, not unkindly. "So? You think I live in a palace? Why would I care about how nice your flat is? Come on, where do you live?"

Estella paused to consider the unexpected turn of events. Jasper and Horace would be out until later in the evening. They liked a good lark about on a day like that, sneaking a little dip in the Serpentine as the evening drew in and the crowds started to leave the park. It would give her the time she needed with Peter without her having to explain him to her friends or vice versa.

"How about I meet you at the Camden Town tube station and we can go together from there?" she said. "It's a bit hard to find."

"Done. See you there at three o'clock."

Estella hurried back to the Lair and made herself presentable, which required trying on six outfits and doing her makeup four times. She made an attempt to clean up the Lair, which mostly involved shooing the bolder mice back into the openings in the wainscot and strategically placing books in front of the most gaping holes. She paced back and forth, arranging the suit on a table, then on her bed, then finally back on the mannequin.

She left the Lair a full hour early to get to the tube station, which was only a few minutes' walk away, just over the Regent's Canal and down the Camden High Street. Camden was not as well-heeled as Chelsea, where Magda and Richard lived. The street was lined with greengrocers and some cheaper clothing shops, along with plenty of stalls of second-hand tat. But it was a bright, vibrant day, and everything looked better bathed in sunlight.

Peter came out of the tube station entrance, a bit late but looking better than she had ever seen him. He was dressed in a simple white shirt and light brown trousers, nothing special. (She would fix all that.) She could see the musician in him, in his stride and stance: his arms had a wide, natural swing, his fingers were long and there was a rhythm to his movements, like he was listening to the beat of his surroundings and walking in time.

"Hello again," he said.

"Hi." There was a pause as they took each other in, and then Peter's face broke into the lopsided grin that made Estella's heart skip a beat.

"Shall we?" he said.

They began to walk, Estella leading Peter back up the Camden High Street, over the canal. "So are you ready to do the show?" she asked.

"Getting there," he said. "We get to play two songs. We're definitely doing 'Everybody's Sun' since it's the single. We don't know yet which other song to do. But the album is selling well. It's in all the shops. I heard John Lennon listened to it and liked it a lot. Don't know if that's true..."

"Of course it's true," she assured him. "It's a good album."

"Well, as long as you like it," he said with a sidelong grin.

A few minutes later, they stopped by a fence that surrounded a vacant plot.

"Well, this is it," Estella announced.

Peter looked around. "What's it?"

"Where I live."

Most homes had doors. That fact was taken for granted. The Lair didn't have a door, because the Lair was not a house, nor an address. The Lair was a place, a hideout, a refuge. As such, it had no number and no doorbell. And no front.

"This is a fence," he pointed out.

"We have to go through it," Estella explained, peeling back one of the loose boards. "Head down. Watch your shirt. There are some sharp bits."

"I admit," Peter said as he bent low to squeeze through the opening, "this was not quite what I was expecting."

"If you liked that," Estella said, "then you'll love this."

She indicated a large hole in the ground, which was partially covered by some wood, exposing an old set of steps that led down into what had been the building's basement. The bomb that had taken half the building had destroyed the first three steps of the staircase as well.

"It's best to lower yourself in," she said, sitting on the ground and easing herself onto the steps. "And hold the rail tight."

Peter looked down into the hole, where Estella was waiting. She assumed he was going to leave, for sure. No pop star was going to follow her into a literal hole in the ground.

But then he sat on the edge and hopped down onto the step.

"In for a penny," he said with a shrug. "Lead the way, Mad Hatter!"

The steps leading down were fairly secure, being concrete, and there was a bit of light from above. Once they reached the bottom, though, it was almost pitch black.

"You might want to stay close," she said.

"Cheeky," he replied.

Then he slipped his arm through hers. She almost staggered at his touch.

Estella had made that trip thousands of times and thought nothing of walking through the dark, decaying pit. She knew every crack, every pillar, every wall. She guided Peter along, glad for the darkness. He couldn't see her wide-eyed panic.

Relax. Just keep going.

On the far side of the basement, there was another set of stairs. The first flight was all right, as they were the same concrete as the previous set. This brought them to the ground floor of the old building. It wasn't bright by any means, but there were a few hints of light through the boarded-up windows. Peter detached himself from Estella but remained close.

"Now where to?" he asked.

"Up," she said.

The next set of stairs was made of wood. Those stairs, while still technically functional, were not precisely up to scratch.

"These can be a bit tricky," she said. "Follow me and only step on the ones I step on."

Estella took Peter up and up, flight after flight, making sure he didn't crash through any of the rotting steps. If she focused on keeping him safe, she could distract herself from the reality of what was going on – that he was following her, that he was here, in her home.

Up, up, up.

"How many more flights?" he asked.

"Almost there," she called back.

They had finally reached the very end of the staircase, where a small hatch led to the gently sloping roof. Estella pushed it open, revealing blue sky. Peter had stopped cracking jokes about the journey by then; he was far too confused.

"Down here," Estella said, demonstrating the way to crawl down the roof. It involved going down on one's backside, in a crab-like motion. It was not elegant, but that was the only way to do it. Peter followed, cautiously climbing down behind her until he reached the hole she had stopped at.

"Our door," Estella said, swinging her legs over the

edge of the opening. The drop was only eight feet or so, and below was a dirty mattress.

"Do it like this," she said, pushing herself off the roof and down into the opening. She kept her feet together so that her fall was straight. The mattress had very little give because of the repeated abuse, but she knew exactly how to propel herself forward and land standing. She looked up and saw Peter considering his options. After a moment, he pushed off, but with too much force. That tipped him forward, and he landed hard, first on his knees and then on his face.

Estella stopped breathing as he lay face down on the mattress.

"Are you..."

Peter erupted with laughter and rolled over.

"Whatever you do," he said, "don't tell the posh lot about this. They'll all be wanting one." He started to stand, but by that point, Buddy had become aware of a new person in the Lair and landed a flying tackle on Peter, pinning him down on the mattress and licking his face with ferocious hospitality.

"That's Buddy," Estella said.

Wink, who had been taking advantage of the empty flat to enjoy an uninterrupted nap in Estella's sewing basket, stared at the visitor with his one good eye while letting out a long, complaining growl.

"Wink," Estella said in a warning tone.

Wink continued to protest, albeit quietened. Estella removed Buddy from Peter's chest, allowing him to stand. He rose, dried his face with the back of his hand and dusted himself off.

Peter looked a bit dumbstruck as he took in his surroundings. "Home, sweet home," she said, her airy tone belying her sudden self-consciousness.

Peter made a slow circuit of the Lair, looking at their grim little kitchen with the tower of uncovered bean tins, the grotty pots, the mismatched dishes, the mouldy bread that was still quite clearly going to be eaten, the milk bottles with green and grey fuzz climbing up the insides and trying to make a break for it. He took in the walls, with their ancient, peeling wallpaper that exposed the brick underneath; the exposed beams above, where a ceiling had once been; the dirt; the umbrellas that still patched bits of the ceiling; the occasional hole in the floor that revealed the space below.

Peter made his way to their turntable and examined the record collection.

"Music lovers, I see," he murmured. "Four whole albums. It's not often I get to say that I've provided someone with a full quarter of their record collection."

"We don't... buy... a lot of music."

Record albums were also clumsy to steal, being stiff, square and easily breakable. She did not mention that part.

"How long have you lived here?"

"Since I was twelve," Estella said.

"What about your mum and dad?"

"Never knew my dad. My mum died."

"What happened?"

Aside from Jasper and Horace, no one knew about Estella's family.

"It's not a great story."

"No, I can't imagine it is. But what happened?"

"I got kicked out of school," Estella began. "I was always getting in trouble. It wasn't my fault, the school stuff. I was poor. I was different. They tried to beat me up. I hit back. I was the one who got in trouble, every time. So they kicked me out."

"Sounds like school," he said.

Estella nodded. "My mum always understood me. She knew I should come to London, to make clothes. To be someone. So after I got kicked out, she packed up the car and we started to drive down here to begin our new lives. But..."

She could no longer go on.

"There was an accident," Estella said. "She died."

"So you've been on your own since then?"

"Not on my own. Jasper and Horace live here, too."

"Who are they?"

"They're... sort of like brothers," Estella said. "They found me when I first got to London. After my mum died. They let me come stay with them."

Peter looked surprised. "So you've all raised yourselves?"

"I suppose," Estella said.

"Who took care of you when you got ill?"

"We took – we take – care of each other," she said. "It was a problem when we all got chicken pox at the same time, but we got through it."

"I can't imagine that," Peter said. "I'm close to my mum. My dad not so much. He doesn't think being a musician is a proper job. But Mum loves it. She taught me how to play piano. That's how I got started. She makes me phone her every other day. She loves that I'm in a band."

Well, aren't you fortunate, Estella thought bitterly. Then she banished that unkind thought as quickly as it had come to her. It wasn't Peter's fault his circumstances had been so different from hers. Some people got lucky, and some people made their own luck. Estella fell into the latter category.

Peter seemed to want to change subjects, as though he sensed a shift in Estella's mood. "And this, I take it, is your part of the manor," he said, drawn by the racks of clothing and costumes to Estella's side of the Lair. She followed, watching where his gaze landed. Her sewing machine, her bed... and then the outfit, waiting on its backwards-headed mannequin. The evidence of the hard work that had gone into its construction was all over the floor: the clippings of cloth, the designs, the pinned-together bits of newspaper where she'd made patterns.

Peter walked to the mannequin and reached out to touch the sleeve of his jacket.

"Is this it?" he asked.

"That's it."

He was silent for about half a minute, and then, finally... "Wow."

Just 'wow'. Estella waited for him to elaborate, but nothing further appeared to be forthcoming.

"Is that a... good 'wow'?" she asked.

"It's a... I can't believe it 'wow'. This is for me?"

Estella found she had been holding her breath and released it all at once.

"So you like it, then?"

"Like it?" He turned, and the sun fell over his face in such a way that made him look more beautiful than she had ever seen him. "Of course I like it. Look at it! No one has a coat like this. Not even Mick Jagger or Jimi Hendrix or any of them."

"Try it on," she urged. "Go ahead. See how it fits."

He removed the jacket carefully from the mannequin and slid it on. It fit precisely as she had hoped, tapering just a bit at the waist, the sleeves falling elegantly low, but not too low. "There's a shirt, as well," she said, getting the work in progress out of her sewing box. "I used some antique lace here, for detail around the neck. I still have to dye it."

He held the shirt and looked at it for a long time.

"You made this for me," he said. "I've never had anything this nice."

Estella shrugged, her cheeks colouring at his compliments.

"You know," Peter continued, "the reason I wanted to come to your flat was that I wanted to see where someone like you lived. This" – he waved his hand, indicating the chaos of their surroundings – "makes sense."

"It does?"

"It does. Because no one is like you, so you must come from a place like nowhere else." Suddenly, a mischievous spark came into his eye. "Anyways, we had a deal. I'm ready to pay up."

"The jacket's not done," Estella protested.

"Neither is the song."

He walked across the Lair to pick up Jasper's guitar, which was resting in its usual spot by the hammock.

"Someone has a guitar," he said, lifting it.

"That's Jasper's."

Peter plucked at the strings a bit.

"Out of tune," he said. "But you'll get the idea."

He sat on the hammock and indicated that Estella should join him. She made her way across the Lair and started to sit in a nearby chair.

"No," he said. "Here."

He patted the spot next to him.

Estella lifted herself up and over, then knocked into his side as the hammock dipped down under the weight of both of them. They were pressed together.

Estella found she didn't mind.

She scooted over just an inch or so to give him some room for the guitar, but not too much.

He began strumming. The song was upbeat, his voice bright and clear.

Found her while making a cup of tea
Don't know if she even noticed me
But now that I'm with her she will always be
The magic bean girl

I see her in the crowd with her ginger hair
You never know what she is going to wear
She came out of my dreams
Wearing only baked beans
The magic bean girl

Peter's voice faded out as he strummed a few final

chords, letting the melody trail off. Estella felt him looking at her, eyes searching, but she found that she couldn't express how she felt.

"It'll sound better once we do it properly," he said apologetically. "I wrote it on the piano. I'm going to put an organ under it as well. But that's it. Did you like it? I know it's not—"

"My hair's not ginger," Estella interrupted.

Peter stared at her. "What?"

"My hair's not ginger," she repeated. "It's black and white."

"Is this your way of saying no, you don't like it?" He sounded confused, almost hurt.

"No," she said quickly. "I... I love it. I just..."

"How do you mean black and white?" he asked. "Is this some kind of metaphor or something?"

"No," Estella said again, shaking her head. "It's literally black and white. Split right down the middle. Black on one side, white on the other."

"No one has hair like that."

"I do," she said. "I colour it because... well, because it's black on one side and white on the other."

"So you've got black-and-white hair and you live in a lair." He laughed. "Why didn't you tell me this earlier? Would have made the lyrics a lot easier."

"Sorry."

"Well, you know what I have to do now," he said, setting down the guitar.

"Did I ruin the song?" she asked, cringing. "It's amazing! It's—"

Peter turned even further into her, put his hand on her hair, and stroked it slowly.

No one had ever told Estella what kissing would be like. What was amazing was that she knew what to do. And that his lips were so much softer than she had expected. She felt her whole body slip and melt away.

Then she and Peter were sinking into the hammock and it was ticking slowly back and forth. The heavy, warm air of the Lair cocooned them in its embrace.

Every once in a while, Estella let herself think about when she was just a kid. Sometimes it had snowed, really properly, not like the dirty dustings in London. She had sat at the window, doing her drawings or sewing. The fire was going, and she and her mum had tea and maybe a biscuit if there were any to be had. Her mum sang along with the radio. It was so comfortable, so completely safe and warm.

That was what she felt now. Safe. Warm. Happy. Here, in the crook of Peter's arm.

12

CHANGE COMES QUICKLY

"HELLO."

Estella jolted upright, away from Peter. Jasper was standing by the hammock, his face frozen in surprise and apprehension. She'd been so wrapped up in their kiss she hadn't heard the boys come in. Estella glared at Wink and Buddy: of all the times not to bark, they'd chosen that one.

"Hi there," Peter replied, seeming not at all bothered by the boys' sudden appearance. "Which one are you?"

"What's going on?" Horace said, suddenly looming over the hammock as well. "What's this? Who's this?"

Estella smoothed her dress and hair and attempted to disengage as gracefully as she could. She rose from the hammock, keeping her chin up as she spoke.

"This is Peter," Estella said. "Peter, this is Jasper..."

She indicated Jasper, who folded his arms over his chest, his gaze locked on Peter's still-prone form.

"And Horace."

Horace didn't respond, in a state of open-mouthed confusion.

"Peter," Estella continued after a beat of silence, "is in the Electric Teacup."

"The what?" Horace said.

"It's a band. The band. That album over there." She pointed at the album, which was leaning against the little table where the record player sat.

"But why's he... *here*?" Horace asked at length.

"A good question," Jasper said, nodding.

Sensing the thinly veiled hostility in Jasper's tone, Peter at last lifted himself slowly from the hammock and hopped out in one fluid motion.

"Estella was showing me a suit she made for me," he said. "We were just having a chat about it."

Jasper said nothing in response, just looked at his guitar, which was on the floor. He pointedly picked it up and returned it to its proper place.

"Well," Peter said, looking back and forth between Jasper and Horace, "I've got to get to rehearsal. I should probably go." He paused. "Then again, I'm not exactly sure *how* to go…"

"I'll show you out," Estella said quickly.

They began the trek, Estella leading the way once more. Getting out was mildly more complicated than getting in, as they had to ascend through the hole via a ladder and climb across the roof. It was madness, how they lived, Estella thought, suddenly fuming. Never mind the fact that Jasper and Horace's display had left her so embarrassed she could barely speak.

"That was certainly something," Peter said once they'd emerged onto the streets of Camden. "Your flatmates didn't look happy."

"Well, we don't really talk about where we live," Estella said, her tone apologetic. "Now that you've seen it… I'm so sorry."

"Don't be," he said, cupping her face in his hand. "I'm glad I at least got to see it once. It helps me understand more about you, and maybe less." Peter smiled. "We'll meet somewhere else next time."

Next time. So there would be a next time.

He leaned down and kissed her, right there on the pavement, in full view of the world.

"Keep me updated, Magic Bean Girl."

"I will," she called after him as she watched him start down the street towards the tube. Then she turned back to the patchwork building she called home.

When she returned, Horace was sitting at the table, Jasper in the recently-vacated hammock. Estella walked nonchalantly to her sewing table as though nothing out of the ordinary had just taken place.

Jasper spoke first.

"Well," he said. "Anything you want to tell us?"

"No," Estella replied, keeping her tone neutral. "Why?"

"You brought him here, Stel," Horace said, joining in. "To our lair. You brought someone here."

"He wanted to see it," she said, shrugging, trying to act like it wasn't a big deal. Of course it was. She knew that. But if she acted like it wasn't, maybe the whole thing would go away.

"But no one comes to the Lair," Horace continued. "That's the point of the Lair. It's our secret."

"Who cares?" Estella protested. "Who's he going to tell?"

"We care." Estella had never heard that tone in Jasper's voice before, so hard and cold. "This is *our* house, where we're safe. We don't bring other people here because it's secret."

"It's not like it was a rule," Estella grumbled.

"Course it's a rule! And you brought him here without even asking us."

Estella felt Cruella stepping out of the shadows. She had heard the commotion and sensed she was needed. Estella tried to hold her off, but Cruella pushed her way into the conversation.

"I don't need *your* permission to show him where *I* live," she snapped. "I don't need to ask if I can bring someone to my own home. We have a lot of what we have because of *me*. Because of what *I* do. *I* sew the disguises. *I* make the plans."

"Plans like what ended up getting us almost nicked at that hotel," Horace said.

"Besides," Jasper added, "what do you think you're playing at, anyways? Rock stars? Rich people? These people don't care about you."

"Yeah," Horace said. "You think you're better than us because you have these posh friends?"

"No," she said. "I think I'm better than you because I *am* better than you."

Silence echoed around the Lair.

"Well then," Jasper said, his voice now ominously level, "if you are so much better than us, then why are you here?"

Estella wanted to back-pedal, to get out of this. Cruella had gone too far, and there was no stopping her now.

"Good question," she said instead. "Maybe I shouldn't be." She gave a short, nasty laugh. "This place is a dump. I try to make it better, but how can I, with you? You're... dirty. You both smell."

Go away now, Cruella. Stop. You're ruining everything. This is too much.

"We don't smell," Horace said meekly.

"So what are you suggesting?" Jasper said. "Are you going to leave or something?"

"I am." *No, Cruella, no.* "I'm going to phone my *friends* and let them know."

Estella grabbed some change and climbed up the ladder, her heart pounding. She returned to the phone box outside and picked up the receiver, her hand shaking. Was she really doing this? Abandoning the boys who had been her family since she was twelve years old, and asking people she hardly knew if she could just... live with them?

Why not? It was how things went in Swinging London. Estella would show Jasper and Horace she didn't need them. She'd land somewhere better, and they could just watch her rise from afar.

She dialled the number Magda had passed to her a while back and waited, her breath catching in her throat. She watched a boy pushing a cart of bottles down the street. That was her reality: broken buildings and old bottles, not—

Magda finally picked up.

"Hello?"

Estella cleared her throat.

"It's me," she said. "Estella. I—" She gulped and tried

to keep her voice breezy. "My flatmates are being *horrid*. I wish I had somewhere else to stay."

"Stellar! Stay here!" Magda said brightly. "What fun! Yes, you must stay with us. We've got heaps of room. Come at once."

Estella felt a rush of relief. So much for Jasper's thinking people like them couldn't care about someone like her. Estella walked back slowly, not sure if she was ready to return and do the thing she had set in motion, but also knowing she was too stubborn to do anything other than see it through to the end.

When Estella re-entered the Lair, she found that there was money spread out on the table in three small piles.

"Still planning on going?" Jasper asked.

She should just say sorry. Undo it all right then. That was all it would take. Jasper and Horace had seen Cruella before. They understood. *Just say sorry. Say it.*

"Yes," she said.

Or not.

"Right, then. Your share," Jasper said, sliding her a stack.

Buddy was looking up at her, his little head tilted to the side in confusion.

She bent down and rubbed his face gently. "You should stay here with Wink," she said to him softly, stroking his matted fur. "I'll come and visit, okay?" She had never gone anywhere without him, but she suspected Magda and Richard would not welcome a new furry companion with open arms. Especially one without a pedigree.

Then Estella packed up her bags with her designs and what clothes she could carry, wrapped a boa around her neck, and left the Lair without a backwards glance.

Estella decided to spend some of the money she had just been given on the nearly impossible luxury of a black cab. It was an expense she had never in her life managed to justify even if she had been able to afford one after a good score. It was like burning money.

But she couldn't show up on Cheyne Walk sweaty and flustered, having dragged her possessions from a bus stop. The whole arrangement had to be executed carefully and with a degree of style. Nothing pathetic and sad. She would turn up like she owned the place.

A short – and extremely comfortable – ride later, Estella marched up to Magda and Richard's front door, tossed her boa confidently over her shoulder, and strode through. She brought the bags (they were so tatty) into the cool, dark foyer, where the grandfather clock was sounding its big, hollow tick. The eyes of the Moresby-Plum ancestry looked down their two-dimensional noses at her from the walls of the staircase. *Pauper,* they seemed to be saying. *What's an urchin like you doing in our home?*

"That you, Stellar?" Magda called from the sitting room.

Estella set her bags down and went to greet Magda, who was in her normal place on the floor cushions, paging through a magazine.

"Do you think this dress is any good?" Magda asked. She pushed a magazine in Estella's direction and pointed at a yellow mini dress with large white circles on it.

"No," Estella said without a moment's hesitation.

"Thought so. Yes, it's clearly ghastly. I do like yellow, though. Betty!"

Betty appeared in the doorway.

"Yes, Miss Moresby-Plum?"

"Make up the blue room for Estella, won't you? She'll be staying with us now."

"Of course," Betty replied, retreating into the foyer. Estella offered Betty a grateful smile that she wasn't sure the housekeeper caught.

"Come on," Magda said, peeling herself from the floor. "Let's get you settled."

The blue room was on the third floor, towards the back of the house, overlooking the long garden. That was perhaps the most astonishing part of Magda and Richard's existence: they had a garden. Land. Grass. Of their own. In London. It was like having their own park. Freshly mowed tracks bisected the expanse of green, thanks to the daily ministrations of their gardener, and masses of roses and other flowers sent up clouds of perfume into the warm summer air.

The room had large windows that let the afternoon sun pour in. It had clearly been decorated last some time ago, like much of the house. It had heavy mahogany furniture, which was protected by lace doilies. There was an Axminster carpet under the four-poster bed. The mattress hadn't been dragged in off the street; it had been purchased in some lovely, expensive shop. The sheets were ironed. There were no sounds of boys snoring on the other side of the room, no smell of beans cooking a few feet away, no rain coming through the roof and no mice dancing across the pillow.

"It's a bit small and the furniture is an absolute nightmare," Magda said as Estella looked around, "but hopefully it will do."

Estella had to keep herself from barking out a laugh. It would do very well.

"I'll have Betty bring your things up," Magda said.

"Oh, I'll do it." Estella made a move towards the doorway.

"Nonsense. Your day has been a nightmare. We'll make it all right. Have a little rest, or maybe a cool bath? Then come down and we'll talk about all the things we'll do now that you're all ours!"

Once Magda left, Estella flopped down on the bed and looked up at the cream-coloured canopy, then at the little silver clock on the bedside table, the porcelain vases and bric-a-brac, the brass lamps. It wasn't fashionable, but it was quality. It was... solid.

She closed her eyes and listened to the birds twittering away in the garden. Had she really been kissing Peter only a few hours before? She thought of his soft lips, his caress, the shape of his body against hers in the swinging hammock.

Kissed by an up-and-coming rock star and playing house with the fabulously rich. Yes: at last, Estella had come into her own. She had always believed that there was a London waiting for her, one filled with cutting-edge fashion and rife with opportunity, one where she could be the person she was always meant to be. She had asked that world to let her in, and that world had opened the door wide – which meant everything she had always known about herself was true. She was special. She was someone.

Would she miss Jasper and Horace and Wink and Buddy...

She pushed the thought away. She had to shut that door and keep it shut; if she focused on them, she would never go forward. Right now she needed to keep her eye on the prize.

This was the new Estella of Cheyne Walk.

13

THE SECRET DESIGNER
OF CHEYNE WALK

DAYS WERE slippery creatures at the
Moresby-Plum residence.

Estella's morning – or, more often, midday – began
when the sun in the room finally grew too bright to ignore,
waking her from a deep, mostly dreamless slumber. Estella
then slowly crawled out of the lovely sheets and down the
hall to the bath. Magda had loads of wonderful soaps and
bath salts. Estella reclined in the tub, and sometimes Betty

even brought her in a cup of tea and some toast so she could dine while she soaked.

Eventually, still warm from the bath, Estella emerged and joined up with Magda and Richard for the dressing ritual. Magda had taken over an entire box room – a small one, but still a whole room – and filled it with racks. There were rows of dresses, skirts and blouses, stacks of hats, coils of belts and even a dressing table full of jewellery. Richard had a similarly massive collection of clothes – fabulous trousers and shirts, neck scarves, suits of every colour and stripe. Estella advised the siblings on their outfits, and she found that if she said something didn't quite suit Magda, Magda would toss it aside and say, "You can have that if you like." In that way, Estella built up a large new wardrobe. The castaways were excellent, and once she modified them, they were even better.

The trio would finally descend the stairs in their chosen outfits, looking like a mad circus. Betty always seemed to know when that was about to happen, and a new tea tray would be waiting in the sitting room, with thick slices of lemon cake that only Estella ever ate. It seemed that Betty took a liking to Estella, perhaps because she ate every bite of whatever was put in front of her and always remembered to say please and thank you. Every time Estella turned around, there was Betty with another tiny china plate of cake or biscuits or sandwiches. She even understood Estella's love of black pepper on everything and dusted it liberally on ham and cheese and pickles.

Once Magda, Richard and Estella were refreshed and rehydrated, they collectively piled into the car and drove across town to Soho, to the Caterpillar.

Estella began to familiarise herself more with the circle of people who occupied ever-rotating places at their Caterpillar table. Gogo was actually the Honourable Georgette McNeil-Jones-Whistler, the daughter of a viscount. Her family had a castle somewhere. (She was never very clear on where; she might not have known.) She was very sweet, even if Estella quickly realised she didn't have two brain cells in the same postcode of each other. Michael, Magda's sometimes-boyfriend, was vain and spent most of their long lunches adjusting his neck scarves or trying to catch a glimpse of his own reflection in a spoon. He went to Cambridge, so he was only down in London for the summer.

There was Penelope, who looked glamorously bored by everything. Roger, who had wrecked four cars that year alone. Cat, who only visited the group once at the café, and whose family owned a chain of department stores. Pamela, who had got married even though she was barely eighteen; she had a baby named Thomasina Telescope, who'd been given over to the care of several nannies almost immediately upon arrival into the world. They flashed in and out with a wave of their boas and scarves, moving on to other lunches and people and stores and sitting rooms, revolving around Magda, Richard, and, suddenly, Estella, like small sparkling moons orbiting the brighter and bigger sun.

After lunch, there was usually some shopping, or a casual drive, or a walk through the park. They returned in the almost-evening, when Magda read magazines or made endless telephone calls. Richard planted himself in a dark corner of the sitting room and read books, occasionally stopping to stare moodily out the window. Every once in a while he picked up a camera to "go out to get some images". He would come back later and say the light wasn't right or he'd seen this person or that person. One day he accidentally bought a car. As far as Estella knew, this was what being a writer was like.

Betty came by with a final round of tea and sandwiches before she headed home for the evening. The summer days were long, the sun not going down fully until nine or ten. Just as dusk finally approached, everyone retreated upstairs for another round of dressing and preening. They got back into the car to go to a restaurant. They never had to worry about dining alone, because everyone swung around to the same places, and almost inevitably a large party formed, their trio at the centre of it all.

Estella discovered foods she had never known existed. She had her first proper Greek meal, which thrilled her with its lemony flavours and pungent olives. There was Italian food: spaghetti, not from a tin, slippery with olive oil and fresh tomatoes. French fare that was a mysterious paradox, remarkable in its sparseness while simultaneously indulgent, dripping with garlic and cream.

When she first began going to the dinners, Estella ate every morsel on her plate, trained never to waste food, as the next meal was always uncertain. But as her meals with Magda and Richard advanced from occasional to multiple times daily, Estella found herself starting to mirror their eating habits, grazing and picking and declaring herself too stuffed to consume another bite when her plate was still half full.

After dinner, it was time to go out. There was music every night. So many clubs – the Scotch of St James, Revolution, the Marquee, the Bag O'Nails, the Crom, the Speakeasy, Blaises – a constant revolving door of spectacles to choose from. Sometimes Peter joined the group for their late-night revelries, his hand on Estella's hip, his voice in her ear, stolen kisses in dark corners. Those were the best nights, when Estella spotted him advancing towards her through the crowds of spinning, dancing souls, making her world stop before he vanished back into the dark so Estella wondered if he'd ever even really been there at all. Things in this new life happened like that – in flashes, at once both brilliant and impermanent.

Their nights finally ended sometime near dawn, when Estella crawled into her cool, clean sheets, made up anew every day by Betty. Vowing to knock out some sketching in the early hours of the day, Estella fell asleep the moment her head hit the goose-feather pillow, only to wake up late the next morning and start the process all over again.

"Morocco," Magda was saying when Estella walked downstairs late one morning. Magda was sitting on the floor in a silk robe, sipping a cup of tea and talking to Gogo, who was playing with a wind-up toy monkey she'd picked up somewhere.

"I've been to Morocco," Gogo replied, nodding. "On the way to Switzerland once. My father knows the prince."

"That's Monaco, darling."

"Oh, yes. Monaco. Morocco is in Africa, isn't it?"

"That's right," Magda said, a patronising note in her voice.

"I'd love to go there. I think my father might have a house there as well. Does my father have a house there?"

"Not sure, darling."

"Well, he has houses all over. I must remember to ask him."

Gogo wound up the toy monkey once again and smiled as it clapped its little cymbals together.

"They have lions in Africa, don't they?" Gogo asked.

"Yes," Estella said, moving up behind the girls and pouring herself a cup of tea.

"I had a lion once," Gogo went on. "His name was Lorenzo. Daddy got him at Harrods. He lived out in the garden but then we had to give him to the zoo, because he tried to eat one of the neighbours. That's what Mummy said, anyway." She shook her head, tresses flying. "I don't think Lorenzo would have ever tried to eat the neighbours. I was ever so sad, but then I got a new horse instead, which is really better, because you can ride a horse, but you can't ride a lion. Not very well, anyway. They don't like it."

Magda continued flipping magazine pages throughout the story, showing zero outward reaction to Gogo's somewhat nonsensical ramblings.

"Tiny thing," Magda said to Estella. "We need the house today. Can you go out for a bit?"

That was a confusing change in routine.

"What about the Caterpillar?" Estella asked.

"Not today."

"What's going on?" Estella tried not to show that she was rattled.

"You'll see," Magda said with a wicked smile. "Come back around six."

Estella got dressed and headed out, alone, feeling oddly adrift, which was silly – it hadn't been that long since she'd had to entertain herself. She wandered the streets for a while, poking around the boutiques and the street markets, then at last settled in the park and pulled out her sketchbook.

She felt a sort of catharsis as she worked through designs that felt like they'd been gathering dust in the corners of her mind for ages. When was the last time she'd sat down and drawn properly, with a vision, with purpose? The whole point of hanging around with Magda and Richard – though Estella could admit to herself that she'd lost sight of the larger objective – was to advance her career with the right crowd, but her fingers hadn't touched a sewing needle since she'd moved in with her friends. Estella made a vow to be more committed to her design work, even if it meant missing a party or lunch.

When Estella returned to Cheyne Walk, feeling refreshed and renewed, Magda was waiting by the door.

"Close your eyes," she said to Estella.

"What?"

"Close them!"

Estella closed her eyes. She felt Magda take her arm and lead her into the house. They walked through the foyer, past the sitting room. They hadn't walked back quite as far as the kitchen when Magda turned Estella to the left and led her down a set of steps that, even with her eyes closed, Estella knew she hadn't been down before.

At that point, Estella cracked her eyes open, because Magda was not very careful as she guided Estella along. That wasn't really Magda's fault; the stairs were terribly narrow and ancient.

"Open!"

Estella did as Magda commanded. She found herself in an old space that probably once had been used solely by servants, with cabinets built into the walls and only a few high windows bringing light in from street level.

The room had been filled with sewing equipment. There was a brand-new sewing machine, the absolute latest model. Two large tables for cutting and laying out material occupied the centre of the room, surrounded by boxes and boxes of things like pins and needles and thread and chalk. There were multiple pairs of shiny new cutting scissors. Several antique-looking lamps had been brought in to provide loads of light.

"This has been sitting empty," Magda said. "So I thought if you're staying here, you'll need a place to sew. I don't know anything about sewing, so I called over to Harrods and they sent a lovely man over with everything you'll need. And I know you love Liberty fabrics, so I phoned them as well and got a few bits."

She turned Estella around. Behind them were rolls and rolls of fabric. Estella walked to them in a daze. Silks, cottons, velvets... so many patterns. All for her.

"I had them send a selection," Magda said. "To get you

started. You can pick through and if you need others, they'll bring them round."

Estella turned back to Magda in disbelief. "This is for me?" She pictured her magical atelier, the one she daydreamed about. This came very close.

"Well, you'll be sewing for the Teacup now, won't you? And you won't mind knocking together a few of your wonderful creations for us, I hope? Richard loves that jacket you made for Peter, and you know I simply love your dresses, so..." Estella felt a smile spread across her face. It was like Magda had been in the park that afternoon with her, listening to her thoughts as she promised herself to recommit to her work.

"I—I don't know what to say," Estella stammered. "No one has ever done anything like this for me before."

"Come now, darling, don't be a sap. It was nothing! And you can say thank you by making me something fabulous to wear to hear the Zookeepers play tomorrow night." She turned to go back up the stairs as though she hadn't just given Estella the singular greatest gift she'd ever been handed. "Let's go get some supper. I'm starved."

And just like that, Estella became the in-house designer of Cheyne Walk.

It turned out that everyone had taken an interest in her work. Gogo wanted a dress with a feather collar. Penelope asked for a cape. Michael wanted a shirt. The entire Electric Teacup needed clothes, of course. (Estella made sure that none of them were as good as Peter's were going to be.) Magda and Richard needed to be completely outfitted. Before long, it seemed as though all the freshest of London society were lining up to be her models. They traipsed down into her basement studio, one after another, for measurements and fittings. She could have any materials she wanted for her creations, and they wore anything she made and told everyone she had made it.

Soon, instead of sleeping late and lingering over lunch and shopping, Estella was at her sketching table before nine, a cup of tea in hand. Richard drove her to Liberty or the Chelsea Antiques Market to buy fabric and lace, old buttons and silver braid. She snatched up old military uniforms and brought them back to cut them apart and reconfigure them. Her imagination ran wild. There were no limits to what Estella could do.

As summer wore on, the heat intensified, and everyone around Soho and Chelsea knew there was a new designer somewhere in town, someone so exclusive that she had no address, no store, no label. Her only calling card was her unmistakably unique, irreverent style, which graced the forms of the young, rich toast of the town. You had to know someone to get to Estella, and Magda and Richard guarded her fiercely.

The only point on the calendar – the only specific time at all – was the upcoming appearance by the Electric Teacup and the completion of Peter's outfit. The other clothes Estella could almost make in her sleep, but Peter's outfit got her full attention. The teapot on the back of the jacket was an absolute masterpiece of silk and satin, with the tea running down the arms now playfully caught in the cuffs of the sleeves. Up to the very last night before their appearance, she was working away, putting the final stitches in place.

On the day of the show, things started happening early on Cheyne Walk. Estella woke to the sound of people coming and going. Magda had insisted on hosting a 'little party' in honour of the Electric Teacup's television appearance, which would cement Estella's status as designer to the stars.

By the time she ventured downstairs just after ten, the supplies filled the whole vestibule, almost blocking the stairs. Estella leaned over the rail in shock, craning her neck to take it all in. It was like the Harrods food halls had been shot out of a cannon directly through the front door. Crates of champagne. Prawns on ice. Packets of little sausages from the butcher. Large boxes of strawberries from the market. Cakes, bread, stinking wheels of Stilton, stacks of Coca-Cola bottles, cucumbers and pickled onions in jars, pineapples, oysters, bacon, prunes, Scotch eggs, meringues and great bushes of mint and borage.

Betty was lugging a crate of prawns to the kitchen when Estella appeared.

"Morning, Miss Estella," she called up. "I just have to get some of these things into the refrigerator before I do your tea."

"I'll do it," Estella said. She opted to climb over the banister, as there was no way of getting down the steps. She headed to the kitchen, where Betty had already made progress, setting out pyramids of glassware and stacks of plates.

"How many people are coming tonight?" Estella asked as Betty set the prawns down by the sink.

"Miss Moresby-Plum said maybe twenty, but you never know. Sometimes they have a hundred in here."

By the time Magda and Richard woke and came down around noon, Estella had brought Peter's suit and the other items of clothing for the band up into the sitting room, for fear that she would get blocked into her sewing room in the basement and forgotten and Peter would have to go onstage in his sad brown trousers and white shirt.

"Oh, good," Magda said, sauntering into the room in a crocheted mini dress. "The things have arrived. Betty, you are a darling and a genius. I hope this isn't a pain for you."

At that moment, Betty had just finished cleaning up after a jar of pickled onions had accidentally been smashed, and she looked like she felt neither darling nor genius. She looked like she needed a cold bath and a nap.

"It's no problem, Miss Moresby-Plum," she said.

Magda took her time pouring herself a cup of tea and then ambled to the telephone, her little gold address book in hand.

"The keys to the kingdom," she said to Estella, holding the book aloft and waggling her eyebrows. "All my secrets. Time to make the invitations."

Estella stared at Magda, dumbstruck. It seemed that she

hadn't told anyone there was to be a party that night, despite ordering enough food and drinks to feed a hundred people.

"You mean no one knows about tonight?" Estella asked.

"Of course not. You don't invite in advance," Magda explained, wrinkling her nose in distaste. "Things like this are just supposed to *happen*." Her gaze landed on the band's clothes, which Estella had carefully laid out on the sofas. "They're brilliant, Stellar! When are they coming by?"

"At four," Estella replied. "Peter said they have sound check at six o'clock, and then the show goes live at eight."

"Marvellous! That gives us some time to have a spot of lunch, and then we'll decorate." Magda clapped her hands. "Tonight will be a *sensation*!"

14

THE MARVELLOUS PARTY

ESTELLA WAS helping Betty haul the crates of drinks out of the vestibule – Magda stretched out on the cushions on the sitting room floor, exhausted from all the telephoning she had done to pass around news of the gathering – when, at half past four, a colourful VW minibus pulled up in front of the house. The Electric Teacup tumbled out and tripped along the path to the door.

"'Ello, 'ello!" Chris strode in first, dressed in a rose-pink shirt and a pair of brightly striped trousers. "We 'eard someone here makes clothes!"

"You made my trousers tighter than his, right?" Peter said to Estella by way of greeting as he leaned down for a kiss.

"In here!" Magda called. "Come see what we've made for you!"

This carried the faint suggestion that Magda had helped in the creation. Whatever the case, Estella was in too good a mood to let the remark bother her. And perhaps Magda had helped, insofar as she had provided the space and materials.

The band fell a bit quiet as they took in what Estella had prepared for them. Tom, the bassist, was given a shirt made of Liberty fabric in a brown Art Deco pattern. Charlie, the drummer, got a black-and-gold jacket with a gold scarf. Chris got an intentionally subdued, but still expertly made, shirt of green satin.

Peter, of course, got the full star treatment: a suit of indigo velvet with the teapot pouring tea stitched in satin on the back of the jacket. She had added gold braid and small epaulettes to reflect the current fashion for antique military wear.

"Well," Chris said, standing back to look at Peter's outfit, "someone got the best one."

Estella was pleased by the jealous annoyance in his voice.

The sitting room was given over to the band as a changing area. They didn't bother to ask Magda or Estella to leave; they simply stripped down to their underwear and put on their new clothes. Magda, of course, didn't react in any way. Estella, blushing furiously, looked down at her lap as they changed, perhaps sneaking just a glance or two up at Peter.

"How do we look?" Chris asked, spinning and preening in his new outfit.

"Groovy," Magda said. "Simply marvellous."

Estella looked up at the four band members she had outfitted, happy mannequins, grinning and posing. They looked like stars.

She walked around them and spent a few minutes examining each outfit up close. All her measurements had been perfectly accurate, her choices for colour and cut ideally suited to each band member. She made a few small adjustments as she inspected them – the tuck of a shirt, the straightening of a collar. Chris needed a belt, and the overburdened Betty was sent to Richard's armoire to retrieve a selection for review. When these did not satisfy, Estella went to Magda's dressing room and brought back an armload of belts and scarves.

"This one," she said, handing Chris a wide brown leather belt. "And you need this..." She draped one of Magda's silk scarves around Tom's neck and tied it in a loose knot.

"Brilliant," Magda said.

Estella went to Peter last while Magda and the other band members stole off to the kitchen for a quick bite. Of course, Peter's outfit needed little adjustment. His had been tried on in advance, worked out in every detail. All she had to do now was tidy the lace front of the shirt, making sure every fold was precisely where she wanted it to be. She stood before him, her eyes and hands working the lace but her attention on the warmth coming from his body. He was looking down at her as she worked. He placed his hands on her arms and gently rubbed them up and down, making her shiver.

"My magic bean girl," he said.

There was no one else in the world right then – just her and Peter in the dimly lit sitting room, with belts and scarves and discarded clothes on the floor around them. Everything she cared about was in that moment – her creation, her...

Love?

"All right, you two!" Chris said, bounding into the room with a sandwich in either hand. He skipped up to Peter and Estella and poked his head between theirs. "I'm the police," he whispered. "This is a raid."

Peter smirked and kicked him playfully. Chris jumped back, waving his sandwiches around. "I've been attacked by our guitarist!" he shouted. "Society is coming to pieces!" He fell to the floor, rolling on the clothes. He dropped his sandwiches, which were mashed into the carpet and discarded items from the fitting.

"Your clothes!" Estella cried, trying to pull him up.

"It's time," said Charlie, standing in the doorway of the sitting room. "Shift it."

Chris popped up from the floor and dusted himself off, following the others towards the door. Peter reached out to stroke the side of Estella's face. "I'll know if you're watching," he said.

"Of course I will be."

He gave her a slow smile. Then the band, nearly manic with energy, tripped outside, back into their van.

"Right!" Magda said, coming into the room and looking at the mess of clothes and sandwich on the floor. "So much to do. Bet-ty!"

The beleaguered Betty, her face covered in a sheen of sweat from the preparations, appeared in the doorway.

"Yes, Miss Moresby-Plum?" she said, slightly out of breath.

"Can you tidy this up? Estella and I are ever so behind."

"Of course, miss," Betty said, her face falling.

"I can do this," Estella said quickly, reaching for the clothes.

"Nonsense," Magda said, hooking her by the arm. "You need to get ready. We both do. Our job tonight is to be fabulous. Come, come."

Estella let Magda lead her up the stairs while Betty gathered the remains of the fashion show from the floor.

There followed two hours of intense beautification. Magda and Estella retired to their separate cool baths, Estella loading hers down with so many fragrant bath salts that she almost bobbed in the water. She rubbed herself with Magda's bath scrubs, which scraped her terribly during the process but did leave her skin fresh and soft. She washed her hair, which badly needed to be recoloured; the black and white was almost starting to peep through. She wrapped her locks around large curlers and spritzed them with orange blossom water. When her hair dried, she let it hang loose in thick waves.

Of course she had chosen her outfit in advance. Estella had opted for a bright blue mini dress – one of Magda's cast-offs. It really was fortunate that Magda would wear outfits only two or three times. Maybe four if they were *very* special. Estella's wardrobe was now so large that it had expanded out of the blue room's armoire and spilled onto the chairs and the floor, then down to her atelier in the basement.

The dress – a gorgeous little number from Biba – Estella had completely taken apart, recut and reassembled into a far superior version of the original. Over the dress she added a satin cape of her own creation, in a rainbow of green, pink, blue and yellow, which attached to the shoulders with buttons. When she turned, the cape flew out around her, transforming her into a wild spinning top. For her makeup, Estella had originally plotted out an elaborate eye design with tiny jewelled appliqués. At the last moment, she ditched the entire idea. Her face, she decided, needed to be almost bare. A hint of blush on her cheek, and a kiss of pale pink on her eyelids. A whisper of mascara, but no liner. Pale pink lips with a little gloss.

Almost bare. Almost herself.

"Was that one of mine?" Magda asked as she and Estella met in the hall. She pinched up some of the cape fabric from Estella's outfit in her fingers. "You *do* have a way, don't you?"

Magda had gone for one of Estella's new creations – a vibrant red catsuit, like something Emma Peel from the Avengers might wear. She'd added a low-slung silver belt that wasn't quite right – there was a black one that would have worked better – but Estella let it pass. That night she needed to be the perfect one.

"You changed your face," Magda commented as she looked Estella over. "Why?"

"It just felt right," Estella said.

Magda turned and regarded herself in the hall mirror. She had put on a heavy cat eye, with stacked black and white eyeliner and duck-egg blue all the way up to her eyebrows. She made a light 'hmmm' sound under her breath.

There was something about it – a strange tone, like something was being decided. Then she turned with a broad smile.

"No matter," Magda said. "Much to do. Come along."

Once downstairs, Magda busied herself with placing joss sticks everywhere and lighting them, filling the house with the obligatory clouds of incense. Estella instantly began to cough and sneeze, following Magda discreetly, pinching out every other one and tossing some of them out open windows.

Gogo arrived first, in a mad mini dress made of small metal circles. It clinked as she moved.

"Oh!" she said, sweeping in and immediately getting herself snagged on a fuzzy coat that hung on a stand by the door. "I hope I'm not late. I forgot today was today."

"You're right on time, darling," Magda said, leading her to the sitting room.

Gogo plucked a strawberry from a platter by one of the couches and began sucking on it, staring at the dark television. Richard, who had been absent for most of the day, suddenly reappeared in the forest-green suit Estella had made for him. It was far too warm for it; the heat of the day hadn't abated at all. The windows and doors were all left open, and soon the house was full of people and flies and the orange cat Estella had named Lucy, who had crawled in one day through the kitchen window and promptly taken up residence in the house, and who now strolled around, helping herself to slices of ham and cooked prawns. The house, which was empty at six, was packed at six-thirty. Estella could barely make her way to the sitting room, and when she did, there was no space on the floor for her to sit. She squeezed into the room, trying to attach herself to a conversation, but none were especially inviting:

"... well, Mary Quant said the bust is dead, but clearly *Angela* didn't hear that..."

"... San Francisco is the real scene, of course. We were going to go there to drop out for a while, but we had to go to Ascot first..."

"... I want to love everyone, but some people are simply too ghastly. How does one love a *bus driver*..."

The funny thing was by then Estella had met almost everyone there; at least a third of them were wearing something she'd made. Instead of greeting people, though, she mentally said hello to the clothes. *Hello, hot pink mini. Nice to see you again, scalloped velveteen trouser suit. Hope you've been well, teal waistcoat with silver fringe.*

She looked for Magda, but her friend was nowhere to be found. So Estella left the room and circled the house, pretending to be on her way to a group of people who were expecting her.

The hour of the programme was growing close now. Estella returned to the sitting room, where someone had switched on the television and the entire party had packed itself in. Estella ended up standing on a small table at the back of the room so she would be able to see, impatiently shuffling from foot to foot as the show went through the various acts. It was unclear when in the hour-long show the Electric Teacup was set to perform. It turned out they were last, so Estella spent most of that hour on the table, willing everyone to shut up.

"Shhh! It's time! It's time!" Estella shouted when the band was at last announced.

The group quietened a bit, but as soon as the camera turned to the band, a loud and echoing whoop from the partygoers went around the room. The programme's set consisted of a series of platforms, with blown-up photos of dancing people. Peter was just behind Chris and to the right, and Estella could catch only glimpses of him, the camera trailing Chris when he moved in that direction. The clothes turned up well on the television cameras, and as they launched into "Everybody's Sun", Peter spun round, revealing the back of his jacket and the magnificent teapot and teacup.

Magda found Estella in the back of the room and joined her on the little table, slinging one arm loosely around her waist. Estella worried for a moment that the table might not hold them both, but she was too entranced to really care. *Let it collapse.*

"He's a star," Magda whispered into her ear. "A star!"

It was true that Peter was coming out as he never had before. Though he still mostly looked down at his guitar and only occasionally out towards the cameras or at the audience, his face was all confidence and lopsided grin. He was beautiful. The camera pulled focus from Chris and turned on him, drawn by the aura he was sending out into the world – and perhaps, to an extent, by his fabulous outfit.

"You did that," Magda said, nudging Estella. "Star. Star, star, star."

Then the song was over. The audience in the studio clapped, as did the audience in the sitting room.

"We'd like to do a new song," Chris said. "It's called 'Magic Bean Girl'."

Estella let out a small gasp. There it was. Her song.

Peter took centre stage, swapping places with Chris, and began to sing. The camera focused on him, and she knew he was looking right at her.

After the television segment ended, the party exploded out of the sitting room and into every part of the house and out into the garden. Estella paced from room to room, nibbling at some crisps and sipping a Coca-Cola. The band would be coming back there at some point. No one knew when.

She encountered Gogo, who had tucked herself into a corner of the room and wrapped herself around the container of a large potted palm.

"I understand your frustrations," she was saying to it. "I think you should be outside, as well. I'll speak to them about it."

Finally, Estella heard a whoop from the back garden announcing the band's arrival. She squeezed through the kitchen and out the back door. The band must have sneaked in through the neighbour's garden and hopped over the wall for fun.

There had to be a hundred people in the garden. They had taken the cushions from the floors, and some from the sofas, and were stretched out and lounging on every part of the grass. Estella stepped into the mass of people, bottles, empty glasses and discarded prawn tails and strawberry stems.

"We have arrived!" Chris said before doing a half-hearted tumble across the grass.

Estella saw Peter following, smiling as he caught her eye. He kept his gaze on Estella as he greeted a few people, making his way across the lawn towards her.

"Oh, hello again," he said as he reached her. "Happen to watch anything good on telly tonight?"

"No," she said innocently. "I don't watch television."

"Very wise. I hear it rots your brain. Now, where can a thirsty fellow find something to drink around here?"

A bottle of Coca-Cola materialised in his hand, provided by some passing person.

"Ah, very convenient," he said. "Now, I'd love to tell you more about my sudden rise in fame and fortune. I know just the place."

He hooked her by the arm and led her to a dark corner of the garden, where they both sank into the grass.

There was no discussion. She leaned in to him as he leaned towards her. Their kissing grew fervent, fuelled by the excitement of the evening, the noise, the music. They fell back onto the ground and rolled into each other's arms. Estella could hear the party going on, laughter around her, the occasional breeze of people stepping over them.

They leaned up for a bit on their elbows for Peter to have a drink. The pulse of the Beatles' "Sgt. Pepper's Lonely Hearts Club Band" was thundering across the lawn.

"Well," Peter said, "a successful evening, I think. Wouldn't you say?"

Estella drank it all in: the soft night air, the smell of the flowers. She didn't want to acknowledge how special the night was, for fear of jinxing it away. She wanted to savour the moment, to hold it still, as if freezing a butterfly in mid-flight. She surveyed the scene in front of her:

Chris leaping around the lawn like a mad sprite.

Gogo dragging the potted palm to freedom.

Magda laughing, the sound like a tiny ringing bell.

Richard taking pictures of the ground.

Jasper and Horace scooping up handfuls of cheese and pineapple from a tray.

Wait.

She felt a jolt of horror and jumped up from the ground.

"Where are you going?" Peter asked. He hadn't spotted Estella's old flatmates, or if he had, he hadn't remembered who they were from that one disastrous meeting at the Lair. Estella closed her eyes briefly, picturing that same meeting playing out with Magda, Richard, Gogo, Penelope... all her new friends.

No. No, no, no, no no. Not tonight. Not now.

"Back in a second!" she called out gaily, as though she hadn't a care in the world.

Jasper smiled as she hurried up to them.

"What are you doing here?" she whispered fiercely.

"Seems like there's a party on," Jasper said casually. "Door was open. People coming and going."

"Were you just *hanging about* outside?"

"We was out for a walk," said Horace, the voice of reason.

"A constitutional," Jasper added. "Like I said, door was open."

Estella narrowed her eyes at them. "What are you playing at?"

They both shrugged.

"Cheese and pineapple," Horace said, helping himself to more of the snacks. "Love a bit of cheese and pineapple."

"Both of you," she said, her voice low, "follow me. Now."

Estella grabbed each of them by a hand and pulled them through the crowd, back into the house and through the twists and turns of the ground floor. They managed to snag bottles of Coca-Cola and handfuls of prawns and Scotch eggs as they went.

Once Estella had them out the front door and on the pavement, she crossed her arms and nailed them with a look that told the boys they were in serious trouble.

"Look," Jasper began, "we just want to meet your friends. That's all. See what this Swinging London's all about."

When put like that, it was not really that unreasonable a request. What harm could it do if they just hung out at the party? There were loads of people there. Horace and Jasper had even dressed up a bit; she felt a pang of unexpected homesickness as she saw that they both wore the neck scarves she had made for them. They had tried.

And she had missed them.

But then her eyes roved over them again, and she started. Something wasn't right. Horace was gripping his sleeve, and Jasper was holding his elbows close to his body.

"What did you do?" she asked in a low voice.

"Do?" Jasper replied.

"What did you take?"

"Oh." He reached into the lining of his jacket. "Three

wallets, some kind of silver thing that was sitting and gathering dust, nothing much."

"You stole?" Estella said quietly. "From here?"

"Oh, come on," he cajoled. "You know they won't miss it. We only took wallets from obvious prats."

"Prats," Horace affirmed.

"These are my friends," Estella snapped.

"*We* are your friends," Jasper shot back. "Those people? Are spoiled and stupid."

"Those people have style," she said, correcting him. "They are smart. They are interesting."

"There was a girl having a conversation with a potted plant."

Estella waved her hand in dismissal. "That's Gogo and she does that."

"And they have style, do they?" Jasper asked knowingly. "Where'd they get those clothes? I'm guessing you had something to do with that."

"Give me the wallets," she said, reaching out her hand. Horace backed away.

"I don't get it, Stel," Jasper said. "Nothing special about them at all. Is it just that they have money? Anyone can have money."

"Not anyone, and that's not even it – not really," she said shortly. "Give me the wallets. Now."

"Shan't," Jasper said, playfully skipping back. "Not until we see our old Estella. These people make Cruella come out. It's not good for you."

"I mean it."

Jasper and Horace began dodging around, weaving between the cars parked along the side of the road and ducking behind trees. They were laughing, but Estella was not. She pointed at a tall, helmeted figure approaching from down the street.

"There is a policeman," she said. "You have ten seconds to get out of here before I call him."

"You wouldn't," Horace said.

"Ten."

"Stel," Jasper said, the grin fading from his face. "Come on, now..."

"Nine."

"I think she means it," Horace whispered.

"Eight."

"Come on, Stel," Jasper said. There was a pleading look in his eyes she had never seen before. "Just come home."

"Seven."

"Jasper, come on..."

"Stel won't call a copper on us," Jasper assured him.

"Six."

"I think she will," Horace whispered.

"Never." Jasper's face hardened; a glint was in his eye.

"Five."

"Come on, mate." Horace tugged at him. "She's got these new ones now. She don't need us no more."

Jasper folded his arms over his chest.

"Four," Estella said. Her heart was pounding.

"I'm off, then," Horace said. "Cruella's here. I don't see Estella anywheres. Come on, Jasper. Come *on*!"

"Three."

Jasper took one final look at Estella – a hard, searching look.

"You know they aren't your friends," he said, his voice quiet.

Two. One.

"Police!" Estella screamed. "A thief! Stop, thief!"

Jasper's eyes widened. He gave her one long, disappointed look and took off running, Horace right on his heels. They were two retreating figures in the night, leaving Estella alone on Cheyne Walk.

Estella stared after them. She'd been bluffing, as it were. It wasn't a police officer; it was just a guy coming to the party in a mad old helmet. Jasper and Horace wouldn't have been able to tell the difference; they wouldn't have known that some guys had started wearing antique military gear for fun. They didn't know fashion. This world was not for them.

It was for her, and she was going in alone.

15

THE MARMALADE PROBLEM

"BIT THREATENING out there today," Betty commented the next morning as she dried the plates. "We'll have a thunderstorm, I think. Would you like me to bring you down some tea?"

As much as Estella liked her workshop, it was a bit dark down there on a grey day like that.

"I'm going to work in the sitting room this morning," Estella said.

"Right. I'll bring it in there, then, miss."

The early hours at Cheyne Walk were largely private times for Estella and Betty. They were the workers of the house. Betty listened to the radio as she did the ironing and cleaned the downstairs. Estella made clothes. That day she needed to get a lot done; she was behind.

To be honest, it was a bit grinding at that point. She barely had any time to draw new designs, as most of her clientele seemed to lust only after things she had already made. They simply had to have "that dress Magda wore to the Bag O'Nails, but could you do it in a green?" Her work was beginning to feel less like creativity and more like drudgery. Estella sighed, reminding herself of the opportunity at hand; since the success of the Electric Teacup's television appearance, her work had been more in demand than ever. And the more high-profile, high-flying youth wore her designs, the better, whether the designs were inspiring to make or not.

Estella settled herself in the sitting room with her materials. Lucy curled up beside her, the cat often making a habit of seating herself on the back of one of the stuffed chairs and watching Estella as she sewed or drew, sometimes treating Estella to a frantic search after she'd grabbed spools of thread and hidden them in the garden.

Magda came downstairs sometime just after one, wearing a pair of hot pants and a matching blouse Estella had made for her. She flopped onto her pile of cushions and flipped through the post that was sitting on the low table where Betty had placed it. The Moresby-Plums had people to take care of all the bills and legal matters, but occasionally someone had the audacity to send something directly to the house, which sent Magda into small fits of terminal inconvenience.

"Idiots," she complained, waving around several envelopes. "I've told the lawyers that these shouldn't come here, but no one listens." She heaved a sigh. "I suppose I'll have to call them again."

"That's awful," Estella said, without looking up from her work, because that was the expected response.

"I know. It's getting so dull around here. I phoned Michael this morning and he was just a dreadful bore. Just going on about all of his thoughts in real time, how much he cares about me. He made it all so tedious. Penelope wasn't home – no idea where she's off to. There are no parties tonight. It's all so *dull*."

Magda tossed the letters back onto the table, then, pouting, stretched out her long legs and stared at her toes.

"What did you do before you came here, Stellar?" she asked. "You had to have an exciting life when you weren't hanging around with us."

"Pretty much what I told you," Estella said, trying to concentrate on a particularly delicate bit of stitching. "We hoisted things. I made clothes. Mostly I hoisted things to make clothes."

"That seems romantic," Magda said. "I'd like to be a hoister. Is that what you call it? A hoister. An East End bird with a nickname, like Mad Magda or something like that."

Estella didn't bother to point out that she didn't think *hoister* was a word; she'd lived in a bombed-out building in Camden, not the East End; and she hadn't gone by a nickname. It wouldn't make a difference – not when Magda got like this.

"That's what we should do today!" Magda said, suddenly brightening. "We'll go hoisting!"

Estella put down her sewing and stared at Magda, whose face was now alight.

"It's not that simple," Estella said.

"Why?"

"Well, there's things to learn."

Magda nodded as though that was obvious. "So you'll teach me. Someone taught you, right?"

"But you don't *have* to steal anything," Estella pointed out.

Magda tipped her head to the side in momentary confusion. "I know that," she said. "But it seems so magical. That's how we met – you were stealing at Liberty. You're in our world. I want to see yours. Come on. It'll be our project."

Estella could see that the die had been cast. Now that Magda had the idea, this would be the course of action. There was probably no harm to it, she considered. Peter was rehearsing all afternoon. It would rain. And Estella could use a break from her production line.

"All right," Estella said, trying to sound half as excited as Magda.

Magda clapped her hands.

"Brilliant! Where will we start?"

"Here," Estella said, motioning around the sitting room. "We don't start in a store. We start here."

"Like a classroom for stealing?" Magda laughed. "What a gas."

Stealing. A gas. Estella resisted the urge to roll her eyes.

Just when she thought this world couldn't do anything else to surprise her.

The first thing Estella had ever stolen was a pint of milk.

Milk was a good way to start. Milkmen left the glass bottles on stoops in the early morning, and no one was ever going to suspect a child carrying a pint of milk of being up to something; all one had to do was pick it up before the homeowner did. Milk was also a basic necessity. When one started with something fairly essential to survival, like milk, it became much easier to move up the ladder and take other things fairly essential to survival, like money or clothes or sewing machines.

The challenge here was there was nothing the Moresby-Plums needed to steal in order to survive. They didn't need food or clothes or money. That left Estella with a bit of a problem in terms of explaining the basics: *Don't get caught, because you can't get caught. Take the food so you can eat. Take the clothes so you have something to wear. Take the money so you can buy food to eat and clothes to wear.* Estella had to admit that nothing quite tickled her like going bigger, taking the impossible, getting close to the floor walkers and escaping at the last moment. But it wasn't just a game, not to her, though there was always an element of risk and chance to it.

Estella went into the kitchen and grabbed a variety of things – forks and spoons, a tea canister, a jar of jam and a salt shaker in the shape of a cat. She brought these things into the sitting room and began arranging them on the middle shelf of a set of bookshelves that stretched the length of the room. It was the same method Jasper and Horace had used in her education.

"All right," she began. "This is what we're going for, right here."

She pointed to the jar of blackberry jam.

"Keep your eye on it," she said as she walked to the far end of the bookcase. She walked down the row, reaching out and touching several items, examining them, putting them back. She lingered on the tea tin, holding it for a moment longer, having a good look at it, before putting it down and walking away slowly.

"And there we go," she said to Magda.

Magda looked back to where the jam jar had been. It was gone. Estella reached into the depths of a trick coat she'd made one afternoon when she'd been feeling a bit homesick, and produced the jar of jam.

"I was watching you!" Magda cried, incredulous. "That's what I want to do! Show me that!"

Estella placed the jam back on the shelf and started to retrace her movements.

"First, you move slowly," she said while demonstrating. "Don't stand in front of anything too long. Keep moving. When you find the object you want, focus on something else. For example, I want the jam, so I focus on the tea."

She picked up the tea again.

"Make sure you can be seen holding it. That's key. Meanwhile, down here..."

Estella turned a bit so that Magda could see what her left hand was doing while her right hand held the tea. Estella lifted the jam from the shelf, careful to keep the coat close to her body. The jam instantly disappeared.

Magda gave her high, trilling laugh. "It's a gas! Show me again. I want to do it. Let me do it."

Estella removed the coat and handed it over to Magda, who leapt up off the cushion and copied Estella's movements. She walked delicately along, examining the wares Estella had set out. Then, with a swift, decisive motion, she turned and plucked the tea canister off the shelf.

"I study the tea canister," she murmured out loud. "And with my other hand…"

With a graceful turn of the wrist, she lifted the jam jar off the lower shelf.

"You're a natural!" Estella said, impressed despite herself. "So elegant!"

"Years of ballet lessons," Magda replied airily. "Dreadfully dull, but I knew they had to be good for something. Tell me, where would you normally go, if you were stealing today?"

"Somewhere busy," Estella said. "Since it's tourist season, somewhere like Harrods, where it's crowded and there's lots of objects all around. A big business like that, they almost expect a certain amount of theft. It's not like when you're stealing from a small store."

"Then let's go there," Magda said.

Estella thought that sounded like a terrible idea. "I thought you just wanted to see how it was done?"

"Well, look how well I did! What fun is it if we don't try it? Come on."

"I only just showed you one basic move," Estella said.

"It takes time to learn." A long time, in fact: it had been weeks before Jasper and Horace had loosed her into a real heisting scenario, where there was no room for error.

"Don't be a drag," Magda said, her eyes turning disapproving.

That was the first time anyone had accused Estella of not being any fun, and Estella did not like it at all.

"Fine," Estella said. "We'll go to Harrods."

First they had to dress.

Estella outfitted Magda with a simple blue shift dress with a secret lining. The dress was not as commodious as the coat, so they had gone over the range of items Magda could take: a chocolate bar was ideal, or a small sampler of Harrods tea bags. Magda then had to accessorise: a large hat, a pair of silver sandals, several bracelets, a massive necklace. Estella had to dress in a complementary outfit, of course, so she paired a silver miniskirt with a gauzy blue blouse. Once they had made sure the hats and purses and shoes all went pleasingly together, they had some cake and tea, Magda made two phone calls, and then, finally, they set off in a big black cab for Knightsbridge, as Richard had taken the Jag and Magda didn't feel like driving the Mini.

Estella looked at the vast department store almost anew as they drove up the street. It looked magnificent in the sunlight, its terra-cotta tiles and Art Nouveau swirls seeming organic and alive.

Sure, she thought as a doorman opened the cab door for them, she was coming to steal, and she was bringing someone who wanted to steal and didn't need to steal. But Magda was also the kind of person Harrods was happy to have. She had money. Loads of it. That meant she knew how to walk into a store like she was supposed to be there, like they should thank her for crossing their threshold. They were two fabulous young women, the smart set, Swinging London itself. Just having Magda within their walls – even if she was taking things without paying for them – automatically raised Harrods' profile.

"Remember, small," Estella said to Magda as they pressed into the store, swept up in the mass of humanity. "Thin. Inexpensive. Common. Something from a pile or a box where one won't be missed."

"Small and thin. Yes. Right hand tea, left hand take."

"Don't linger. And never run."

Magda giggled.

Now that Estella was back in her element, she felt herself getting into the spirit. It had been far too long since she had lifted something. She was going to lose her touch if she wasn't careful. The two stepped deeper into the food halls. There was, inevitably, one of the endless groups of tourists milling through.

"Here," she whispered to Magda. "Watch this."

She took off her hat and waved it in front of her like a fan.

"It's so hot," she whined out loud.

As she did this, she reached over with her right hand and relieved a man of his watch. A moment later, the watch was hidden inside her hat, which went back on her head. She smiled at Magda, who burst into laughter.

"Confidence," Estella instructed. "Calm confidence."

That was when she saw the head of her old friend, the red-faced security guard, bobbing along in the crowd, like a hairy beetroot. Normally, she would turn away at his approach. This was a different day in all ways.

"Walk away from me," Estella muttered to Magda out of the side of her mouth.

Magda looked between Estella and the guard with

curiosity. "That man is staring at you like he knows you."

"Oh, he knows me," she replied, "which is why he'll be watching me, not you. Walk away from me like you don't know me. Now. Now's your chance. Go get something."

Magda turned gingerly on her heel and went one way while Estella walked directly towards the man. When he saw her approaching him, his gaze narrowed.

"I thought I told you not to come back here."

"I'm just a shopper, sir," she said politely, and louder than necessary. "Why are you talking to me? Mummy, Mummy, this scary man…"

She looked around frantically as if searching for a parent. Other shoppers turned and stared at the guard, who flushed and stepped back without ever taking his eyes off Estella. She slowly backed away until she had a good distance between them, and then she casually walked towards Magda, who was standing by a display of jams and marmalade with a dumbstruck look on her face.

"I did it!" she whispered. "I did it! Oh, but I couldn't get my hand in the inside pocket, so I put it right here." She motioned towards the sizable jam-jar-shaped bulge in the dress's front pocket. Instead of getting the nice, flat chocolate bar, Magda had reverted to the practice item – the heavy, easily seen practice item.

"No," Estella said, trying not to panic. "No, not jam. It's too large. It's got 'Harrods' on the label. You've got to get rid of it. Now. Put it back."

The guard, possibly smelling blood, started in their direction.

"Oh!" A gleam came into Magda's eye. "He's coming over! He's coming over!"

"Put it back," Estella said again. "It's not stealing until it's out of the store. Just put it back and we'll walk away."

Magda did not put it back. Instead, she started running, the one thing Estella had insisted that she should not, could not do. She broke for the door, pushing past people as she went. Estella swore to herself and hurried after her, shoving through the crowds of people who bumbled around the doors, blocking the way. They reached the vestibule between the inner and outer doors to the department store.

"Magda!"

By then, Magda's expression was no longer one of pleasure or excitement. She had a genuinely petrified look. She bolted for the door to the outside, which was being held open by one of Harrods' green-coated doormen. Estella tried to linger, to buy Magda a few more seconds, but the crowd nudged her out as well, pushing her onto the pavement. Magda stood there, her face blank. She pulled the jam out of her dress pocket and shoved it into Estella's hand.

"Get rid of it," she said.

"Magda! I can't—"

But the guard was upon Estella, and then she was on the ground, holding Harrods property in her hands: one jar of lime marmalade.

Everything moved slowly for a second. Estella saw Magda bolting off, glancing once over her shoulder as she went. The clot of tourists shifted in confusion. There were heavy hands on her wrists. She thought about trying to pull free, but the effort seemed pointless.

Sometimes when you were nicked, you were nicked.

16

WHEN YOU'RE NICKED

"BEEN AFTER this one for a while," the guard told the constable, looking extremely pleased with himself as he hitched up his trousers and fixed Estella with a glare.

Estella, the guard and the constable were all in a small room behind one of the counters in the food hall. The guard plunked the jar of lime marmalade on the small table.

"This is all a misunderstanding," Estella said, her voice calm, polite.

"I've had her here before," the guard continued, as if Estella had not spoken. "Pickpocket. Almost got her a few times."

Estella widened her eyes. "But why, sir, would I steal a jar of lime marmalade?"

They all regarded the lime marmalade on the table. For its part, the lime marmalade wasn't talking.

"People steal all sorts, miss," the constable said, though he looked a bit baffled. Estella was well-dressed, well-spoken. And stealing lime marmalade *was* a bit weird – not to mention, all things considered, pretty small potatoes. Not exactly the crime of the century.

Sensing a possible ally, Estella decided to press her luck. "I understand this gentleman is only trying to do his job," she went on, directing her speech to the friendly constable. "This is all so *horrid*. I came in with my friend. We were shopping. I think she picked up the marmalade by accident. She's very absent-minded. I had no idea she had it. As we were leaving, this man came up behind us. My friend realised what she was holding and had a bit of a panic. She pushed it to me and ran. She must have been petrified."

Estella was getting the tone and patter down. She'd

placed an emphasis on *horrid*, and she saw the constable take it in.

"I almost had you a few weeks back," the guard growled.

"I'm ever so sorry," Estella said. "I don't know what you mean. I can pay for the marmalade. Here..."

She made a show of opening her handbag – or rather Magda's handbag – which was of a very fine quality. Everything about Estella suggested that she was not someone who would come to Harrods to steal.

The constable sighed. "Perhaps just a misunderstanding here," he suggested to the guard with a meaningful look. "A prank, perhaps? The young lady here seems quite contrite, and I'm sure she'd never do anything like this again."

Estella nodded vehemently in response.

"I'm telling you, I've been trying to get this one," the guard repeated. "She's always worked alone before. Must have a partner now."

Estella wanted to say, "Yes, I do have a partner now. We're part of that new criminal enterprise that's trying to steal all the jam jars in London one by one. We're playing the long game." But she resisted the urge, remaining silent and allowing her lower lip the most delicate quiver.

"How old are you, miss?" the constable asked.

That was always a tricky question. Too young and they might try to get parents involved and discover there were no parents. Too old and they could arrest you and put you in with the adults. In this case, Estella thought it was probably best to be honest.

"Sixteen," she said.

"Perhaps a telephone call to her parents will sort it out," the constable said.

"They're on holiday," Estella said, improvising. "In Morocco. I'm staying with my friend's family. My friend will be in ever so much trouble! How ghastly for her!"

The situation now required a bit more emotion. Estella summoned up some tears, just enough to moisten the eyes. She wasn't talented enough in the art of fabricated crying to manage full-on bawling. That would have been overdoing it, anyway. The misting was enough to make the constable visibly unsure of himself.

The guard, however, rolled his eyes.

"Hang on," he said. "Keep her here. I'll show you."

Estella didn't like this development. What could he be getting? She spent the lapse in action making sure to look pitiful, dabbing at her eyes. The guard returned within a minute with the salesperson from behind the seafood counter.

"Remember her?" he prompted the seafood man.

The seafood seller regarded her for a moment. Estella sniffed.

"Oh yes," he said. "She was in here a little while back. The one you chased out."

"You're sure?" the constable asked.

"Oh yes. Bright ginger hair. I remember you, love."

The guard rolled back on his heels smugly. "It's her," he said. "Must be part of a gang now. And she had stolen property."

Estella felt the blood drain from her face. The tears came more easily now.

"I've no idea... I was just here with my friend!"

"No, that's definitely her," the seafood seller said, almost as though speaking to himself. "I used to have to do some intelligence during the war. Got to be able to know faces well, never forget 'em."

Estella questioned that internally but on the outside continued to look confused and pathetic.

"All right, then," the constable said. "We'll just walk over to the station, I'll phone your friend's family, and we'll get to the bottom of this. You're not going to try anything foolish, are you?"

"She'll run," the guard warned. "You can take her in one of the Harrods vans. I'll have one sent around."

Truly, Harrods was the store with everything. In this case, a signature forest-green van with the gold Harrods logo on the side, used to deliver a sixteen-year-old lime-marmalade thief to the police station.

Lime marmalade. It was so beneath her that Estella was tempted to remove her hat and show them the watch that was still sitting on top of her head.

Estella was curious, in spite of her precarious circumstances.

It was, remarkably, the first time she'd ever made it that far in the nicking process. She'd been spotted before. She'd had to run. She'd slipped away from grabbing hands, talked and cried her way out of situations, ducked around corners. But she'd never had to sit on a bench in a police station while a Woman Police Constable, her dark hair pulled into a low, severe bun, stared at her over a cup of tea and filled out a form with a dull pencil.

"Name?" the WPC asked.

"Paulette McCartney."

"Try again."

"Gibbertine Fairywagon."

"How long are you planning on doing this?" the woman asked, sounding more tired than truly peeved.

Estella shrugged.

"They brought you in from Harrods," the WPC continued. "Stealing lime marmalade? What was it, a prank? Was it supposed to be funny?"

"I didn't steal it," Estella said. It was true, after all.

"Let's try again. Name?"

"Elizabeth Windsor."

The woman sighed and set down her pencil.

"All right, you," she said. "If that's how you're going to be, you're going to have to go in the cell."

Minutes later, Estella found herself in a holding cell, a small whitewashed space in the back of the station that smelled of carbolic soap and old sick. The only furnishing was the hard bench built into the wall. Estella sat on it and considered her situation, some of the curiosity at the newness of her predicament having worn off and been replaced instead by abject annoyance. Magda must have seen her taken down by the security guard, and yet she'd continued to flee, never stopping to think she might help Estella get out of what Magda had got her into.

Estella knew what she would have done had the positions been reversed; she would have waited and watched, and if Magda had not turned up soon, she would have gone to the police station to help her sort it all out there.

That was what Estella had thought would happen for a while, even after she'd arrived at the station without Magda or Richard in sight. She held out hope that they would still show up; they had plenty of money to pay any fine, after all, and surely Magda would be worried about her.

The hours ticked by. Estella curled up on the hard bench and tried to get some sleep, but the lights were on and she wasn't tired or comfortable, and she was more than a little hungry. At some point, she was aware that it had to be night time. The people coming into the station were louder and drunker and were put into holding cells around her. Several other women landed in Estella's cell sometime during the night. One of them shook Estella awake just after she had drifted off.

"Get off," the woman said. "I want this bench."

The woman was much larger than Estella, and

meaner-looking, and there seemed no reason to provoke her. Estella got off the bench and lay down on the concrete floor, focusing her gaze on the fine cracks, lamenting what a far cry this was from the wonderful bed at the Moresby-Plums' home. It wasn't even the scratchy sheets and creaking bed frame of the Lair.

Magda and Richard would turn up at some point. They might not have known where exactly Estella had gone, but they had people – lawyers and things like that – to do things for them. They called them all the time to get money sent or bills paid or things done. They would shell out money to find her and make sure she was safe; she just knew it.

Soothed by the thought, Estella finally nodded off again, her face pressed flat on the floor. Occasionally she woke and opened one eye to make sure no one was leaning over her. Sometime in the early morning, the cell door opened and Estella and her new associates were all taken out. Estella, dismayed that Magda and Richard had, in fact, not appeared, was plonked down in front of the same WPC as the day before, who took the same dull pencil and attempted to fill in the same form.

"Name?" she asked.

"Belinda Belvedere," Estella said.

The WPC looked doubtful, but it was at least a possible name, so she wrote it down.

"Age?"

"How old do I look?"

"Don't get smart with me," the WPC said. "Now come on. How old are you?"

Better to go up than down, probably. Down would prompt too many questions.

"Eighteen."

"Right. Address?"

"None."

"No address?"

"I'm new in town," Estella said.

"From where?"

"France."

The WPC set down her pencil.

"Come on, then, Belinda," she said. "Time to go see the magistrate."

Estella stumbled into the magistrate's court and took her seat with the other shoplifters, still-drunk partiers and assorted weirdos who washed up on London's shores every dawn. A magistrate, who looked to be about 112 years old, sat at the bench and went through the sheet he'd been handed.

"Belinda Belvedere?" he called out eventually. Estella stood up. "You are accused of stealing a... jar of lime marmalade from Harrods department store. What do you have to say for yourself?"

"A misunderstanding," Estella said. "An accident. I don't even like lime marmalade. I don't think anyone does."

"You may be right about that," he said. "Terrible stuff. Can't imagine why they even sell it." He peered closer at the paper in front of him. "It says here the security guard believes you to be a regular shoplifter."

"The security guard is mistaken," she said.

"Yes, well, I expect he knows his job. But since you've spent a night locked up, I think that will do for a jar of lime marmalade. But if I see you in front of me again, I won't be as understanding."

And with that, Estella was thrust back out into the London sunshine.

It was just after one o'clock in the afternoon when Estella, exhausted and starving, head pounding beneath her hat, finally turned down Cheyne Walk. She'd had no money with her for food or transportation, so rather than risk turning back up at the magistrate for lifting a bread roll or a few pounds for the tube, she decided to walk. The sandals she'd been wearing, a slightly-too-small pair borrowed from Magda, had cut into her feet with every step until ultimately she'd decided to go barefoot.

As she'd walked, Estella had reasoned with the feelings of rage and betrayal that threatened to bubble over once she'd evaded any immediate danger. How had Magda and Richard not come looking for her? How had they left her to rot overnight in a jail cell, especially when the whole disaster had been Magda's fault in the first place? There had to be an explanation.

Maybe one of them had grown violently ill. Yes, that was it – food poisoning from one of the fancy restaurants, probably the one that insisted on serving everything raw. Estella had quickened her steps; she'd get back to Cheyne Walk and find Betty beside herself with her hands in her hair, tearfully relaying to Estella that Magda had been in hospital all night long, with Richard beside her, and that she'd been asking for Estella since the moment she'd woken up.

But when Estella finally reached Magda and Richard's

door, she found no sign of Betty. In fact, she found no one at all. The door was locked, and she didn't have a key. Estella knocked and knocked, but no one answered. She thought about waiting on the step, but she was much too hungry for that.

So she walked on to the Caterpillar, where she knew she would find them.

When Estella entered the Caterpillar, Magda and Richard were there with Gogo and Penelope, laughing loudly about something. The music didn't exactly scratch to silence, but there was a decided quiet that fell over the conversations as she advanced towards her friends' table. A server froze in place, cocked her head in confusion, and slowly retreated back through the beaded curtain. Estella heard a muffled laugh behind her. She knew how she must look: barefoot, hair mussed and askew, outfit dirtied. But still she straightened herself up, tossed back her hair, marched up to the mushroom that served as Magda and Richard's table, and sat down.

"I'm starving," she announced.

Magda, she noted, inched slightly away from her. Richard looked her up and down and turned with sudden interest to a paperback he had on the table. Penelope almost climbed into her handbag.

Only Gogo spoke, gazing at Estella with her large, innocent eyes. "Why do you look like that, Stelly?" she asked.

Someone a few tables away mumbled something. Estella made out the word *stinks*.

"I spent the night at the police station," Estella replied, tossing back her head and smiling like her evening had been one giant party.

Gogo looked confused. "Why? Do you like to sleep in police stations? Is that something people are doing now?" She turned to Magda. "Magda, should we be sleeping in police stations?"

"No, darling," Magda said. She turned towards Gogo, managing to avoid all eye contact with Estella.

"Then why did Stelly do it?"

"Estella stole something from Harrods," Richard said, eyes glued to his book.

What?

Was that what Magda had told him? Estella looked at Magda, who had suddenly seemed to take an interest in her fingernails.

"I didn't," Estella clarified, unable to keep the edge out of her voice. "Magda did, but—"

"Oh, it was all just a lark and it went wrong," Magda said, her tone breezy.

"Yes," Estella said, giving Magda a long side-eye. "A lark that resulted in me spending the night in a police station."

"Yes, well," Magda said, "that's over now. We were just talking about Morocco. I simply have to see the Gettys' house. You know, that's where Keith and Anita got together. She went there with Brian and came back with Keith..."

The server came over and looked at Estella, still visibly confounded by her appearance.

"The usual," Estella said with dignity. She smoothed back her hair, getting a little whiff of herself in the process. The person several tables over wasn't wrong: she did stink. Penelope looked at Estella from under the staggeringly thick coat of black eyeliner she wore and twisted her lips into a little grin. Eyes blazing, Estella stared right at her until Penelope buried her gaze in the depths of her handbag.

An omelette soon appeared in front of Estella, and it took tremendous restraint not to snatch it off the plate and eat it with her bare hands. But as soon as she'd dug in, the conversation seemed to flatten. Magda yawned broadly.

"Time to go, I think," she said, "have a little wander

round Carnaby. There's a darling little jacket I want to get..."
Her voice trailed off as the group stood up, gathering their
things.

Estella paused in disbelief, a forkful of perfectly cooked
omelette halfway to her mouth. "You're *leaving*?" she asked.

"We've been here for hours," Penelope explained.

"Can I talk to you for a moment?" Estella said in a low
voice to Magda, grabbing her arm as Magda trailed by her,
following the others.

Magda gave Estella an odd look but reluctantly sat back
down. "What is it?" she asked brusquely.

"You're leaving when I just got here," Estella said.

"Well, you can't just come into the Caterpillar looking
like that."

Estella, who was more aware than most about how things
looked, felt like she'd been slapped. "I spent the night in the
police station," she said again, speaking slowly. "Remember?"

Magda scoffed. "That's hardly my fault."

"Hardly your fault? You stole *marmalade*. You put it in
my hands and then you ran away."

"I assumed you'd know what to do with it," Magda
snapped.

"I told you what to do. I said nothing large. And not to run."

"If you're going to be *horrid* about it..."

"I got nicked for you."

"I have no idea what that means," Magda said.

"It means you gave me the jar and I got caught."

"What was I supposed to do?" Magda asked dully.

Estella wanted to scream. "Not act like this when I got here!"

Magda shrugged. "You're the thief," she said. "Now, you should go and have a bath and change your clothes. We're going shopping. Here." She pressed the house key into Estella's hand.

"You don't have to give me back the outfit," Magda said over her shoulder as she exited. "I don't know if that smell is going to come out."

After finishing her omelette with as much dignity as she could muster, Estella returned once again to Cheyne Walk, still barefoot, even though by then her feet were sore and scuffed with blisters on the soles. She almost welcomed the pain; it distracted her from her rage.

Estella let herself in. The house was cool and dark, perfumed with the previous night's incense smoke. Betty must have come back from the shops while Estella had gone to the Caterpillar; she poked her head out of the kitchen.

"Oh, there you are, Miss Estella," she said. At least Betty didn't seem fazed by her appearance. Then again, Betty had likely seen so much at that house that nothing surprised her anymore. She probably thought filth was the newest craze. "Do you fancy a cup of tea?"

"I'm all right, thank you," Estella said, trudging to the stairs. The eyes of the Moresby-Plums followed her as she made her way up the creaking steps, pulling the miniskirt and blouse off as she went. She sniffed the clothing, recoiled, and then threw the pieces over the banister. They landed on a bust below.

Estella ran a bath in the biggest of the bathrooms, the one with the luxurious claw-foot tub. She furiously dumped in large handfuls of Magda's expensive perfumed bath salts, filling the bathroom with clouds of rose and jasmine-scented steam, fogging the mirrors. The water was too hot, but she lowered herself into it anyway, embracing the sting. She grabbed a loofah and scrubbed feverishly until every trace of the night before was gone.

Every physical trace, anyway.

Magda had left her holding the bag and then sneered at her? Told her she stank?

Estella stewed in the bath a long time, letting the water grow cold, then draining it halfway and filling it again with hot water. She filled it high, not caring if it sloshed over the top. She heard Magda and Richard come home. She remained still, listening for the sound of Magda's step on the stairs. Magda would come and apologise. She had to.

But there were no steps on the stair, and soon she heard music start up. They put on *Sgt. Pepper* with the volume cranked high. The sounds of John, Paul, George and Ringo drifted up to the bathroom. "Lucy in the Sky with Diamonds" floated in and echoed around the tiles, asking Estella to picture herself in a boat on a river, with tangerine trees and marmalade skies.

No marmalade skies, thank you. She was never eating the stuff again.

Estella stayed in the tepid water as long as she could stand, but after a while she grew cold and her skin was hideously pruned. She got out without bothering to drain the bath, and she made a conscious effort to leave wet footprints trailing down the hall. She went into her room and shut the door loudly, then climbed into the luscious, soft bedsheets and pulled them up to her nose. That was one thing she truly loved there: the sheets always smelled like orange blossoms.

She was so tired. She was exhausted from the night before and upset about how the day had gone. Maybe a nap would refresh her and everything would be better when she awoke, like coming to after a bad dream.

The light filtered gently through the curtain, Estella's eyes drifted shut, and before she knew it, she was waking up on the cusp of evening.

Nothing had changed downstairs except the album. They'd put on the Electric Teacup.

The sleep had restored Estella somewhat. She felt more kindly towards Magda than she had earlier; maybe someone like Magda just truly couldn't grasp what it felt like to spend the night in a jail cell. Estella *had* come on a bit strong at the Caterpillar, practically backing Magda into a corner. And speaking of coming on strong, what had she been thinking, going into a place like that looking and smelling like she had?

Estella had done wrong, but she would make it right.

She had a good thing going there; she wasn't going to let it all break apart over a jar of lime marmalade. She would descend the stairs back to her full, resplendent self, looking better than she ever had. She would remind Magda and Richard that she was their Stellar, practically a part of the family. That was all it would take to restore her to their good graces.

Estella dug through her pieces in progress. Nothing seemed right; nothing was big enough, elegant enough. She'd done dresses out of newspaper and bean tin wrappers and plastic. That night called for something lady like, traditional materials, worn exceptionally well.

The lace curtains from upstairs, the ones she had thought about making into a canopy. She hurried up the steps, past the frozen gazes of the Moresby-Plums, to the boxes of material and removed the curtains. Back in her room, she realised to her delight that the lace in question didn't even need to be sewn. She draped it over her head and shoulders, securing it at the nape of her neck with a pin. To cover the pin and complete the effect, she opened her window and pulled a pink rose off the trellis, then tucked the bloom easily into the lace.

Simple. Beautiful. Delicate. The hood gave her clean,

shining ginger hair an elegant frame, and the cape swept down to her ankles, in contrast to the mini dress she'd put on beneath it. Like a Jane Austen heroine on the streets of London.

It was perfect.

She descended the stairs regally, knowing the effect the outfit would have and almost giddy in anticipation of Magda's warm exclamations and Richard's nods of approval.

Magda and Richard were in the sitting room. Magda was on the phone, as usual, when Estella appeared in the doorway.

"All the best people are going to be there," she was saying. "I heard from Marianne that you can get the most amazing—"

She stopped speaking as Estella entered the room.

"I'll just phone you back," she said, then set down the receiver.

"Have you been home for a while?" Estella said, as though she hadn't been hearing pounding music for the past few hours. "I didn't hear you come in."

"Oh, hours now. Stellar! You look amazing!" Magda smiled as she said it, and her voice was bright, just as Estella had hoped – but there was an odd note in it.

"I know," Estella said simply.

"Is that our lace from upstairs?" Magda asked.

"The lace that was boxed up, yes," Estella clarified. "I thought it would make a good cape."

"It's divine," Magda said, more coolly. "We had Betty bring you up a tray. You seemed exhausted, you poor thing."

Estella waved a hand as if food was the last thing on her mind. "Oh no, I was just fine, but thanks," she answered, matching Magda's distant tone. If Magda was going to be cool, Estella would cover herself in frost.

"I'm going to the Silver Circus to see the Electric Teacup play," Estella continued. "Would you like to come?"

Richard had tucked himself into the far corner of the sitting room with a book and was half buried in colourful cushions. He peered out of his little hiding place. "No," he said. "I don't think so. Might stay in tonight, have some people over."

Estella looked to Magda for confirmation.

"Yes," she said with a thin smile. "I'm exhausted today, for some reason. You still have the key from earlier, don't you?"

Estella smiled stiffly. "Of course," she said. "I'll let myself in."

"You always do, don't you?" Magda replied, turning back to the phone.

17

STONEHENGE

ESTELLA HAD decided it was not only okay but preferable to go to the Silver Circus alone. She didn't need Magda and Roger; she was with the band. She didn't need an entourage; she was already in one.

The venue perfectly suited Estella's mood; there was no better place to escape and let loose than the Silver Circus. It was one of the smallest clubs in town, but the club used that to their advantage, to heighten their exclusivity.

Patrons entered via a small hallway between a boutique and a restaurant near Piccadilly, through a door that had been painted to look like a clown's face, and from there descended to a cramped basement where nearly everything was covered in silver foil, with swinging, spinning lights tinted orange, blue and green forming distorted patterns on the walls and ceiling. Customers lounged in the circus-like seating in the round. A looming cut out of a ringmaster dominated the scene, spinning hoops descended from above, and occasionally a performer came through, jogging on a balancing ball or juggling rings of fire.

Estella descended the multicoloured steps proudly, letting her lace cloak trail loose behind her. She felt like a queen, and when one felt like a queen, others sometimes responded accordingly. The crowd seemed to part and make way as she stepped down to the dance floor and positioned herself close to the stage. The warm-up band was just concluding their set, and the stagehands began setting up the Electric Teacup's drum kit.

Estella had never gone to clubs before her time with Magda and Richard. She had not been a music person. Truthfully, she still wasn't a music person – but by then she understood the scene. Clubs were fashion shows. They were places to see and be seen. If there was a band playing, so much the better.

There was time to kill before the Teacup started to play, so Estella danced to the music that played over the speakers until the next set. She twirled around to the Beatles and The Who and the Rolling Stones. She was getting a little bored and dizzy by the time the lights came up on the stage.

Out they came – Chris leading the charge, wearing his tightest trousers yet and a flaming red shirt. Peter appeared on the side. He wasn't wearing one of her creations, but he had gone with something she'd suggested he purchase – a two-toned suit from Lord John in sapphire blue and violet. It wasn't as good as Estella's clothes, of course, but it was enough to give him an edge. He moved towards the front of the stage. No more hiding behind Chris now.

Estella scooted over so she was directly in front of him, and he smiled down at her and gave her a broad wink. A moment later, he played the first chord of "Everybody's Sun". The crowd let out a strange sound – not quite a roar, but a euphoric hiss. All at once, there was a surge towards the stage. The people who had been so easy to dominate a few minutes before were now a flailing mass. Estella was pressed up against the edge of the stage, unable to move. She couldn't dance or twirl; she was pinned like a butterfly on a board, beautiful and frozen. Chris had his head thrown back and was singing for his life while the band blasted away behind him. Peter's focus was on his guitar, the rest of the band, and, occasionally, the entire audience. He didn't seem to notice Estella stuck against the stage. He was engrossed in his work.

Estella had chosen a fairly delicate shoe for this outfit, but it did have a small heel. She stamped her foot backwards, making contact with what may have been a bare foot. A girl yelped. Estella took the opportunity and forced her way back slowly, step by step.

At last free from the stage, she was caught in the organic movement of the crowd – an ecstatic pulse. Estella let herself go, sliding around, trying to dance – sometimes succeeding, sometimes stumbling. She'd seen the band play before, and people had enjoyed it; this time, people were in an absolute frenzy.

This was stardom.

There was almost an hour of this joyful punishment that

was this intense, frenetic mass of moving bodies. She drifted on the tide, moving all around the room. She was well out of Peter's sight now, caught in the rapture. People accidentally struck each other as they danced; Estella was knocked in the eye with the tail end of a whipping braid, and her feet were stamped so many times that she no longer felt it.

And then, just as quickly as it had started, the music stopped, and Chris thanked the audience. The band left the stage, and the crowd slowed down, floating back to the bar and the tables, or moving gently to "White Rabbit" by Jefferson Airplane. The crew began to clear the instruments. Estella made her way back up to the edge of the stage, looking for Peter. She was not alone in that; several people were gathered, calling out various band members' names, looking to make contact. The crew ignored them all. Finally, Estella saw a hand come out of the shadows and point at her, and a man came to the edge of the stage and helped her crawl up.

"Estella?" he asked. "Come on. You're wanted."

She proudly made her way backstage into the dark of the wings, into Peter's waiting arms.

"Where were you last night?" Peter asked as he escorted her back into the depths of the club. Estella hadn't expected the backstage to be so small, so grotty, just a narrow little area with writing all over the walls, cords and wires everywhere, remnants of sandwiches and empty cups on the floor.

"In jail," she said, snuggling into him.

Peter let out a surprised laugh. "Of course. Come on. Have to pack up."

The band might have been stars onstage, but off it, they still had to clean up after themselves. Guitars, drums, amps – all of it got lugged through the bowels of the club and into a back alley, where the band's VW minibus, roughly painted in swirling red and orange, awaited them. Everything went in – masses of stuff.

Chris had shed his sweaty stage clothes and had changed into a fresh floral shirt and a massive coat in a wine-red shag. "This way, ladies and gentlemen, this way," he said, urging the group into the back of the van.

"What's going on?" Estella asked as she climbed into the van, ducking low to clear the doorway.

"It's a full moon," Peter replied, turning back to look at her with a mischievous spark in his eye. "We're going on an adventure."

Estella felt a pit form in her stomach. She had been on an adventure the day before, and that had not gone well. But... this was Peter. Her Peter. Plus the Electric Teacup, plus Estella, plus two girls she did not know who appeared to be with Chris and Charlie, all piled in – seven people, plus instruments, in a van that definitely could not quite fit them all.

She took a seat on Peter's lap, and he wound his arms around her waist. Tom took the wheel. "Onwards!" he yelled as he fired up the engine. He ground through the gears and the van rocked into life, groaning under the weight of all the people inside. It trundled forward, picking up a bit of energy as it made its way out of the alley and onto the main road.

"Where are we going?" Estella asked Peter.

"Stonehenge," he replied.

"Stonehenge?"

"Yep. Big henge made of stone," he said. "Can't miss it. Biggest henge around."

She elbowed him gently.

"I know what it is," she said with an eye roll, though in truth she knew only a little bit about what it was, having never been. Basically that it was a henge, whatever that was. Big rocks. "Isn't it... very far?"

"Hour or two," Chris said, turning around from his seat in the row in front of them.

Up front, Tom cranked up the radio, filling the van with music as it sped out of London. It was far too loud to talk. She settled into Peter's lap as he tightened his arms around her and sang along with the music. The wind whipped in through the open van windows.

It seemed pretty clear that the navigator had little to no idea what he was doing. Chris was singing and laughing like a madman, sometimes holding a torch in his teeth and consulting a map that rippled in the airflow. They seemed to get lost somewhere near Twickenham and looped the town several times, which led to a chant of "Twickenham again!" as they went round and round. They stopped by Hampton Court Palace so that some of the guys could relieve themselves and Chris could perform a dance by the gate for the ghost of Henry VIII. The petrol almost ran out, but they found a late-night service station near Basingstoke, which resulted in another dance.

The strange journey through the night was rapidly turning into the longest trip Estella had ever taken. England itself went by the motorway. It was too dark to see most of it, but she looked anyway. She could make out the shapes of pubs, the outlines of houses and trees, and open spaces – so many of them. Estella had forgotten the world could be so wide.

Several consultations of the map seemed to indicate that they were hours off course, but that was soon righted. Chris leaned out the window and pointed at Andover, which started another chant, this time, "Andover Andover Andover", which at least made more sense. Then the towns fell away completely, and the VW was bracketed entirely by great rolling plains. The full moon spilled light over the earth, and they could see the great standing stones in the middle of Salisbury Plain. A small frenzy erupted in the van. Tom pulled the van to the side of the road and stopped. The door opened, and the travelling Electric Teacup circus spilled out onto the grass and started running.

"We are Druids!" Chris yelled, holding up his arms. He tore off towards Stonehenge, his great fuzzy coat flapping around him.

Estella stepped out of the van and looked up at the night sky, falling behind the others. In London, even under the cover of darkness, the light was filtered through smoke and smog and city ambiance. Here there was nothing between her and the moon. It was low, so much brighter and bigger than she had ever known. It illuminated the plain with a clear green-blue light, and she could see the white night shadows of the clouds blowing by.

She had seen pictures of Stonehenge in books. It had never looked like much – just some old rocks, some standing and some sitting on top of the standing rocks like door lintels. Now that she was there, on that strange moonlit night, she saw why they held such fascination. They were so lonely and austere. The stones were massive, forming a perfectly imperfect broken circle. The formation spoke to something eternal, something that communicated beyond the veil. This was the place of magicians and ancient secrets.

It was cold. Estella shivered in her thin lace cape. It had been enough for a crowded London club, but certainly not for this.

"Here," Peter said, having reappeared beside her.

He removed his jacket and helped her into it. He took her hand, and the two of them walked along slowly behind the others, who were now closer to the stones.

"What did you mean before when you said you were in jail?" Peter asked. They could finally talk without the constant whistle of the wind whipping through the VW's windows.

Estella shrugged. "I meant what I said. I spent last night in jail."

"Great Train Robbery finally caught up with you, eh?"

"Magda wanted to learn how to lift things from shops. I took her to Harrods. It didn't go well. She took a jar of lime marmalade and left me holding it when the security guard came. I got nicked. I spent the night in jail."

Peter laughed so loud that it echoed over the plain.

"How do you exist?" he asked, his tone incredulous. "You mad, mad thing."

"Magic," she replied, smiling. When he said it like that, she could almost forget the cold, cracked floor of the cell. The whole event took on a faraway, dream-like quality, something that might not have ever happened at all, especially when juxtaposed with this otherworldly night.

"So how did you get out of it? Did Magda and Richard send their cadre of lawyers?"

"No," she said. It was an unpleasant bit of reality on that unreal night. "No one came." At Peter's sidelong glance, she rushed to defend them despite herself. "I talked my way out of it in front of the magistrate. It was only lime marmalade, in the end."

"Still," Peter said, shaking his head in disapproval, "you

don't leave your mates like that. I would have come for you. You should have called me."

She was warm now. It came from the inside and flushed every part of her being.

"I don't really know them that well," Peter continued, "and I know they're your friends. But I've never had a lot of time for posh people."

Estella was confused. "I just assumed they knew you before I turned up."

"No," he said. "They know Chris. And I think they only know Chris because he's met a lot of poshos now that we're on the scene, as it were. As soon as you make it, people with titles and deep pockets come rolling up to your door. Never knew there were so many sirs and ladies out there." He looked into Estella's eyes. "They don't understand people like you and me. And they probably never will."

Estella nodded, letting Peter's words sink in and resting her head against his shoulder as she took in their surroundings. One thing about the place: it was quiet. Estella had never known silence like that, ancient, big silence that stretched over the land. It was just her and Peter. The others were there, gadding about, but she and Peter were alone together in this subdued world.

Peter squeezed her hand harder. "Anyway, I wanted to tell you – we got some news earlier today," he went on. "That's what this trip is about. A little celebration. The appearance on telly the other night – it went really well. The record company is sending us on tour. Twenty dates around England." His face broke into a grin. "Five more in Scotland. And they're talking about sending us to America for two weeks." He let out a soft whoop. "Can you believe that? America!"

"You're... you're leaving?" Estella asked, trying to keep her tone light even as her stomach sank.

"No. Well, yes. By definition, yes. But we're just going around the country. And haven't you always wanted to see America?"

"America?"

"You know, New York, California, whatever other places there are."

Estella squinted at him in the darkness. "You want me to come with you?"

"Well, we'll have to work something out," he said, smiling.

Then he bent down and kissed her. It was soft, because this was not the place for anything more. Still, as his lips brushed hers, she felt something pleasant and shivery travel up her spine.

Estella in America. She had to admit it did have quite a ring to it.

"The ceremony must begin!" Chris announced from above Estella and Peter as they approached. His fuzzy red coat cut a sharp outline against the moon. He'd taken up position on one of the stones that had fallen from the monument, like it was his own personal stage.

"What's he playing at?" Peter muttered, smiling.

Estella and Peter sat down by the stone with the other members of the group and leaned back on their elbows. Estella's mind was still whirling from what Peter had just told her, but they'd have to wait until later to discuss it.

Chris was pacing the rock, his arms high in the air. "We have come to this mystical place to ask the old ones to help us on our journey!" It was at times like this when it was perfectly clear why Chris was the lead singer: he had an innate theatricality, mugging and leaping around.

"We ask you, all ye wizards and witches who inhabit this place, we ask you, King Arthur, we ask you, Gandalf, we ask you, Beowulf, and Bilbo Baggins, and..." He paused. "Er, who else do we have?"

"Winnie the Pooh," called one of the girls.

"Yes! Winnie the Pooh, and Tigger, too! We call upon you. And you—"

"Sherlock Holmes," Tom added.

"Indeed! We call upon Sherlock Holmes, and Ebenezer Scrooge, and James Bond, and the Queen, God bless 'er."

He bowed deeply, and the group all made bowing gestures from their recumbent positions.

Chris continued. "We call upon these spirits to assist us in our journey towards the toppermost of the poppermost, that we may ascend the mountain of fame without falling into the valley of madness, that we earn loads of dosh, that we become the kings of the charts and the kings of the hearts. By Stonehenge tonight, we offer this light!"

Chris patted his pockets for a moment.

"Anyone have a light?" he asked in his normal voice.

Someone tossed over a book of matches. Chris jumped off the rock to grab it, then scrabbled back up and lit one tiny match against the dark.

"Yes!" he cried. "We offer this great flame! This mighty torch! We, the Electric Teacup, ask this of you, old ones! What say you?"

"Get off, yeh prat!" Tom called out in a funny voice. "We're trying to sleep down here."

"I understand, old one," Chris said, his tone solemn as he bent down and held up his hands in a placating fashion. The match went out. He groaned. "Oh, bugger. We lost our torch and I woke up an old one. Never mind! We ask Stonehenge and the moon! Help us reach number one! Number one! All chant now, number one!"

"Number one! Number one!" they all cried. Estella joined in. "Number one! Number one! Number one!"

The chanting went on until Chris spun round and accidentally fell off the rock, prompting a loud cheer from the surrounding group. He flopped comfortably onto the grass. "I think that should do it," he said. "And now, do what thou wilt."

"Don't need to be told twice," Peter said, rolling towards Estella and putting his lips to hers.

18

RUDE AWAKENINGS

ESTELLA AWOKE late the next day back at Magda and Richard's house, in her bedroom. Outside, the day was grey and forbidding. Estella stirred and kicked the blanket away. She was still wearing the dress she had worn the night before, lace cape discarded in a heap on the floor.

The world came back into focus. After Chris's ceremony, the Electric Teacup and company had finally piled into the van sometime around dawn. The drive back was quieter and peaceful. Almost everyone was asleep, possibly even Tom. (They'd been jolted when the van swerved off the road and was righted at the last moment.)

Estella had dipped into and out of a doze as she cuddled on Peter's lap. At one point, she had blearily opened her eyes to see early-morning England going by outside the windows. Beautiful prim homes with flowers in the gardens. She saw the black-and-white Tudor outfittings of pubs and shops. People were pushing prams and going to work. Out in the country, the towns had greens, cricket pitches, proud clocks with benches under them as the major landmarks. She must have fallen asleep completely at some point, only coming to when they pulled up at Cheyne Walk. She'd stumbled inside, up the stairs and into bed.

Estella reached for the little silver clock by the bed. It was almost two in the afternoon.

As she made her way to the bath, she ran into Betty, who was carrying a pile of folded clothes in her arms.

"Oh, there you are, Miss Estella," Betty said brightly. "Didn't want to wake you. I'll get you a pot of tea. Will you be going as well?"

"Going?"

"With Miss and Mr Moresby-Plum?"

"To the Caterpillar? No. Not today."

Betty looked a bit confused, but she smiled. "I'll get that tea, then," she said. "And leave it by the door of the bath."

Estella proceeded to the bathroom and started to fill the tub, idly staring into the sink as the water rose. The sink was made of Dutch porcelain, with a blue-and-white pattern. She had never really examined the picture etched within it until then. It was of a windmill in a field surrounded by flowers. Until the previous day, that tableau would have seemed like something out of a fairy story. But she had seen the fields and the flowers. She had run the plains at dawn. She had been initiated into the strange collective of the Electric Teacup. The whole whimsical world was hers, even the pretty windmill drawing in the sink.

She was jolted out of her thoughts by the loud thunk of something heavy being carried down the stairs. Then another. Then a third. She turned off the tap and peered out to see Betty heaving a great suitcase down the steps, struggling under the weight of it.

Curious, Estella pulled on her dressing gown and followed. As she descended the stairs, she found that the foyer was filled with suitcases. Magda was standing by the mirror at the door, trying on a massive floppy-brimmed brown hat.

"What's going on?" Estella asked.

"Oh, good afternoon," Magda said, turning to greet Estella with a bright smile. "Does this hat go with this dress? I'm just not sure."

"No," Estella said reflexively. Even when confused, she could process clothing questions. "Wear the black one. What's happening?"

"Oh." Magda switched hats. "We're going to Morocco. Marianne called, you see, and there's a marvellous party going over. The Stones are going, and we just have to go. We talked about it before, I'm sure? It's always been the plan, you know. Everybody is going to Marrakech. Almost everyone is already there." She tilted the hat this way and that, trying to find the right angle.

"You're going... now?" Estella asked.

Magda giggled. "Oh, no, silly." She pouted into the mirror. "Not until this evening."

"Oh." Estella sat down heavily on the stairs and let her thoughts catch up with her. "Right. How long are you going for? A week?"

"A bit longer. Three months? Six months? There's Morocco, and we might swing up through the South of France. We'll be back in the spring, I suppose. We can't stay here in the winter. It's far too dreary." Magda turned to look at Estella. "Do you think you can be ready to move out by this evening? We leave at six."

"Move out?"

"Well, yes. It's time to have the place redecorated. You'll have to find somewhere to stay."

Betty came in from the kitchen with a cup of tea, which she passed to Estella through the rails of the staircase.

"Will you be wanting your cosmetics case as well, Miss Moresby-Plum?" she asked.

"Hmmm, yes, I suppose," Magda murmured, already distracted. "And another hat box. I'm taking these along as well."

"Of course."

Estella's mind was racing. How could they just be... going? To Morocco? Now? And leaving her with nowhere to stay? She tried to remain calm. She steadied her hand as she sipped her tea.

Think. Think. What could she say?

Richard came out of the sitting room. He saw Estella sitting on the step, then looked at Magda meaningfully. "We should go to the Caterpillar soon," he said. "Gogo will be waiting."

"Yes," Magda replied. "Of course." She flung the hat off her head and turned. "Leave the key on the table here when you go. It's been ever so much fun."

And then she was gone, leaving Estella sitting alone on the step with her tea.

It was said that England got a good, proper summer for maybe two weeks each year. That year had been generous, with its blue skies and long sunny days. But now the weather had decided it was time to revert to its normal setting – wet, dreary, changeable. The sky was a pale slate colour, and the temperature had dropped. And while it wasn't yet raining, there was a telling, distinctive scent in the air that spoke of torrents to come.

Estella looked out at the gloom through the fourth-storey window of the house on Cheyne Walk. She was alone there aside from Betty, who was far away downstairs, folding clothes and packing them in suitcases. Even Lucy the cat seemed to have moved on. It was just Estella and the room of antiques, which had never been moved or dealt with.

She had been in worse situations, of course. This was

nothing. Nothing at all. It was unexpected; she simply had to think.

Going back to the Lair was not possible. She had ruined that completely. If she showed up there now, Jasper and Horace would chuck her out.

Estella's gaze landed on the jumble of invaluable rare instruments. A light bulb went on.

Peter. Tour. Estella in America.

Of course. He had asked her to go with him. Sure, it was a bit early to join up, but he would let her stay in the Electric Teacup flat. She hurried to the telephone in the upstairs hall and dialled his number, but the line was engaged. She tried several times but could not get through.

What now? She could keep trying all afternoon, but that would eat up time. She needed to talk to him now. The trouble was she didn't have his address.

Magda likely did. Magda knew where everyone lived. She would have it in that little gold address book of hers, the one that was full of secrets.

Estella ran down the steps to the foyer, where the bags sat. Magda and Roger had a lot of suitcases, eleven in all, plus smaller personal bags, hat bags and cosmetics bags. Magda's book had to be in one of them. Estella listened closely to try to hear where Betty might be in the house, not wanting to be caught snooping. It sounded like she was up in one of the bedrooms, from the creak of the floor. Estella opened the bags one by one, rifling through the dresses and dozens of silk scarves, stockings, boas, sixteen pairs of shoes, sunglasses and hats, and the entire case of eye shadows and lipsticks.

Nothing.

She tried Peter's number one more time from the downstairs phone. Still engaged.

"Get off the sodding phone!" she hissed as she clanged the receiver down.

She was going to need the address book, and quick. Magda must have it on her, in her handbag. That meant Estella was off to the Caterpillar, possibly for the last time.

Ten minutes later Estella was on her way to the Caterpillar in a cab for which she'd borrowed spare change lying around the house. She wore a simple dress and little red wellies, plus a sharp white raincoat.

As Estella rode along, she considered the situation. Maybe the problem was that she hadn't exactly explained to Magda and Richard that she *needed* somewhere to stay; it was an imperative, not an option. She had only ever said that her flatmates were being difficult. They had never asked for more than that. If they knew she had nowhere to go, well, that would be a different story. Estella smoothed her hair. She couldn't come across as needy; that wouldn't work. She just had to make them understand.

She arrived to find Magda, Richard, Penelope and Gogo at their table, same as ever. Estella slid onto an empty cushion. Penelope regarded her over her little china cup of tea.

"You're a bit wet," she observed.

"That'll be the rain," Estella replied. She hadn't meant for it to have the hard snap it did. The reply didn't land well. Estella could feel the cloud of her wet, ordinary presence descending over the table.

"Oh, hello," Magda said, regarding Estella almost in confusion, as though she vaguely recognised but couldn't quite place her. "How are you getting on? All set?"

"Almost," Estella lied. She had packed nothing. To be fair, all her possessions would fit in just one of Magda's suitcases.

Gogo regarded her with wide eyes. "Are you going to Morocco as well, Stelly?" she asked.

"No," Estella said as though she was thrilled about it. "I'm staying here. You know, with Peter. And I have designs I'm working on."

"Of course," Penelope said, nodding. But her eye had a nasty glint. "You must be hard at work. Our own Little Nell."

So this lunch was going to go even more poorly than the last. Composure. She needed to maintain it. She tried to look interested in – even delighted by – the group's travel plans. They were all going, from the sound of it. Magda and Richard that evening, Gogo on the weekend and Penelope the following week. There was casual talk of Heathrow, of getting cars in Marrakech, of grand houses and nights under the stars. With every passing moment, Estella became less visible to them. She felt herself fading, no more real than the pattern of the sky projected onto the floor.

As they finished up their ice cream and tea, Estella put on her sweetest possible smile for Magda. "Could I speak to you for a moment?" she said, staying seated. "I want to say goodbye."

Richard sighed impatiently. "I'll bring the car round," he said.

Estella turned to Magda after Richard and the others had taken their leave. "I think," Estella began carefully, "that we both were upset about the Harrods thing. I don't want to leave it like that."

"Oh, it was nothing," Magda said airily, as if she had been the main person affected.

Estella swallowed hard against the wave of unbidden rage that rose within her. "Oh, good," she went on. "I'm glad. And... I was wondering, perhaps I can just stay in the house? Watch over it for you? I could help with the decorating, make sure the painters are doing the right thing...?"

"Oh, aren't you a *dear*? But Betty can take care of that."

"And make more clothes, of course," Estella rushed on. "I have loads of designs I want to make for you. I could really get down to it, make you loads and loads of things for when you return."

Magda waved away Estella's suggestion as though shooing a fly. "Oh, I'm sure we'll get loads while we travel. People have been bringing back divine things from Morocco, and Paris, of course—"

"The thing is," Estella interrupted, feeling more desperate by the moment, "I don't actually have anywhere to stay."

"You have a flat," Magda pointed out helpfully.

"Not any more," Estella said. "I can't go back there. I don't have anywhere to go."

Magda blinked. Estella saw her trying to digest that concept. In Magda's world, there were always places to go. You went to one of your houses. If one wasn't available for some reason, then you simply went to another. There were always spare houses. Barring that, there were villas and hotels. One always had somewhere to go.

"Well," Magda said, shifting the spoon in her empty teacup back and forth. "That's quite unfortunate, but I'm sure you'll work something out."

"Magda. Please," Estella whispered, feeling her eyes fill with tears and hating herself for it.

Magda took a deep breath, looking bored and a little annoyed, like this was all a tremendous bother.

"Listen, Estella, it's been a gas, really it has," she said. "But we run in different circles. You understand. Different worlds. We've had a good summer, but it's probably best we part ways now. Less difficult for you."

"For me?" Estella asked in disbelief.

"Well, of course," Magda said, looking around self-consciously at Estella's heightened tone. "We're meant to be with different sorts of people. It's in our breeding. I'll be married someday soon, having babies, going to social events, and you'll work in a shop or something..."

Estella felt something rising in her as Magda went on about the thrilling high-class life she'd one day lead, contrasted with Estella's low-class, low-grade future. The feeling seemed to come from the very centre of the earth and punch its way through the many layers under London – tunnels and foundations and ancient plague pits. It cut through the floor of the Caterpillar, entered through her shoes, travelled up her legs, and shot up her spine into her head. It felt like the red dye would simply fall away from her hair, and her true locks would shine through.

Cruella was here.

"... anyways, you understand," Magda finished.

"I do," Estella said, smiling so hard her cheeks hurt. Her voice was syrupy sweet. "You'll be hanging about with the inbred half-wits that are your peers. You'll marry some thick aristocrat, I imagine – some dull-as-dishwater bag of teeth and tweed, someone who will have to deal with your utter vapidity and lack of originality. Meanwhile, I'll be working in a shop, as you say – a house of design, to be exact. I'll be making works of art and creating the trends you'll be trotting behind, always trying to catch up and never quite making it. I suppose I'll see you, dragging your weird little children around London. Because by all means, darling, maintain that bloodline. That family tree of yours, well, the branches are quite short, aren't they? And I'll look at you and remember our summer together, when I truly came to understand why mediocrity is a scourge that has to be overcome."

Magda said nothing. Her mouth hung open. Estella reached over and gently lifted Magda's chin with her finger, shutting it.

"Have a marvellous time in Morocco," Estella added.

Before anything else could be said, Estella rose with great dignity, bared her teeth in an approximation of a parting smile, and left the restaurant. She waited until she was well outside before she pulled the gold address book – the one she had taken from Magda's handbag while she was ripping her to shreds – from up her sleeve.

There was no going back to Cheyne Walk now. The rain

had got worse. It stripped the trees of leaves and left the pavements slickly patchworked. Everywhere there were black umbrellas and heads down, people hurrying. Estella put up her own umbrella and pushed against the wind, trying to keep her hair and makeup as intact as possible.

Go back. Punish her some more. Make her hurt.

"Go away now, Cruella," Estella said as she hurried through the darkening day. "Things to do."

19

LOVE IN BLACK AND WHITE

ESTELLA STOPPED under the awning of a record shop two streets over and started paging through the little gold book. There was nothing under Peter's name. Estella groaned in frustration, then paused. *Chris.* That was who she probably filed it under. He was the lead singer, after all, and the most famous one, and they all lived together. Why bother with Peter when Magda could just concern herself with the very top?

Problem was Estella didn't know Chris's last name. But she knew how to find out.

She ran inside the shop and grabbed a copy of the Electric Teacup's album out of someone's hand.

"Hey!" the guy protested.

"Shush. I'm looking for something," she said as she scanned it for the band's full names.

There. Chris Isherhall.

She shoved the album back at the aggrieved shopper and went through the *I* section of Magda's book. Sure enough, Chris Isherhall. Beak Street, Soho.

"So predictable," she muttered under her breath.

Estella had used up all the money she'd taken from Cheyne Walk on the cab ride, so she would have to walk to this address. Luckily, she was already in Soho, but she soon got turned round amid the famously dense warren of streets, alleys, nooks, mews and crooks. She had to stop several times to ask people if they knew the way. Half of them pointed her in the wrong direction, so she was backtracking and turning round as the rain came down harder and her umbrella grew essentially useless, but finally she found herself on Beak Street, looking up at a brown brick building.

The ground floor appeared to be a naughty bookshop.

There was a blank white door leading into the shop, but she couldn't see a way of getting upstairs to the floors above. She was going to have to throw something at the window.

Estella lobbed the address book upwards, making contact on her third try, and caught the book on its way down.

"Hey!" she shouted.

The window above her opened at last. Tom's shaggy head popped out.

"Estella? Is that you?" He peered sceptically at her sodden, crumpled frame.

"Is Peter home?" Estella asked impatiently.

"Peter? He's..." He scratched his head. "Think he stayed at the studio all night. Working on something. He's over there."

"What studio?" she asked, trying to remain patient. "Where is it?"

"Dynamo. It's over on St Anne's Court. Just round the corner."

He pointed vaguely towards the street she had just come from. She took a deep breath, waved goodbye and started running in that direction. The cold cut through her vinyl coat, and she kept slipping in her boots.

St Anne's Court was one of those London streets that,

like the one the Lair was on, had taken a beating during the war and hadn't quite got back on its feet. It was more of a short alley than a proper road. One side was filled by a bit of crumbling wall, the only remnants of a building largely destroyed by a bomb. There was a Chinese restaurant, a laundromat and one small doorway with a sign that read DYNAMO STUDIO. She opened the door and entered a small lobby, where a man with a flushed pink face and a massive bristling moustache sat behind a desk, reading a copy of *The History of Cricket*.

"I'm here to see Peter Perceval," she said.

The man slowly set the book face down on the desk. "Who's that?" he asked, his expression blank. "Band name?"

"From the Electric Teacup."

The man took what felt like three months to put on a pair of reading glasses and consult the clipboard in front of him.

"And you are?" the man said, peering at Estella over the top of his glasses.

"A friend of his."

"Are you, now? What's your name?" The man regarded her with a sceptical gaze.

"Estella."

He looked at the list again, as if he were consulting an ancient text.

"No Estella on here."

"He doesn't know I'm coming." She was trying to keep the impatience out of her voice; she really was.

"Well." The man set down the clipboard. "We don't just let anyone in here, you know. We have all sorts of people trying to get in here to see the bands. Girls, mostly. They try all kinds of things. Try to come in the windows, don't they?"

"Well, I know him," Estella said shortly, wishing she sounded more convincing.

"That's as may be, luv, but your name isn't on the list here." He tapped the list as proof.

"Can you just tell him I'm here?"

"No," he said, rocking back in his seat. "We don't interrupt them when they're working to let them know every person who turns up here. We get all sorts, like I said, all day long. Come here pleading and crying to see the bands. All day long. You're not even the first today. All day every day, they come. We had the Beatles in here one day and you should have seen it. People still come looking for them."

Estella realised that she was dealing with someone who

relished telling other people bad news, and that the man intended to lecture her for as long as he had breath. She considered making a break for it and running down the hall. She could easily outpace him. But that was not a good way to make an entrance.

"I'll just wait for him, then," she said, as though that didn't leave her feeling extremely bothered.

"Ah, well, now, you see, we don't allow that, either. I'd be knee-deep in girls if we allowed that. Against the fire code, at any rate." He shook his head. "No, I can't allow that. You can wait outside as long as you like. Free country and all that. But you can't stay here in the lobby if you don't have business here, and if you're not on the list, then—"

"I get it," Estella cut him off, heading for the door.

She stepped outside into the foul weather. There were very few places to seek shelter. There was a phone box close by that had a good view of the studio. She waited for the person inside to finish his interminable call, banging on the glass with the heel of her hand to get him to move it along, as the rain sleeted off her jacket. He responded with a rude gesture. She banged again and again until he got tired of her and hung up.

"Emergency!" she said when he stepped out. He shook his head but said nothing. Estella climbed inside the booth and shut the door. She was soon both sweating and cold at the same time, her hair sticking to her forehead and her dress clinging to her legs. She had to keep wiping the moist fog off the glass to look out and keep watch on the studio.

A few minutes later, Estella spotted Chris striding up the street, his mane of black hair snapping in the wind.

"Oh, hello!" she said, springing out of the phone box and causing him to jump back in surprise.

"Estella," he said, shaking his head. "What..."

"I'm supposed to meet Peter here," she said, smiling, as if she'd been having the most marvellous day of her life. "But the *dreadful* man at the desk won't let me in."

Chris looked confused for a moment.

"Meet him here?" he said.

"Oh yes. I was nearby at the Caterpillar and he told me to come by when I was done."

Chris paused as though he was trying to puzzle something out, then said, "Right. No problem. Come with me. You'll catch your death out here."

He offered her his arm to link hers through, which was

nice enough. The two pushed open the door to the studio, where the bristle-brush moustache man sat sentry with his beloved clipboard.

"Hullo, Mac," Chris said cheerfully. "Brought a friend here. She's with us."

"Right you are," said the man cheerfully, with no acknowledgement of his and Estella's previous conversation. "Studio four, as usual."

The business end of the studio was a surprisingly mundane-looking place – a blank hallway with a bunch of numbered doors. They opened the door marked 4 and entered a room full of panels of equipment and a massive console of buttons and levers and dials. There was a large window, which seemed to look out onto nothing but the ceiling of a space beyond.

There was sound, though: the lone voice of someone singing in lush, resonant tones to the gentle melody of an acoustic guitar. It was a new song.

When everything's in colour
And everything is bright
I thought love was rainbows
Turns out love is black and white

"He's always writing," Chris said, his tone holding a mixture of scorn and admiration. "Busy boy, our Peter. Good one, isn't it? Sounds like a single to me. What do you think?"

It was a delicate song, and there was something raw and genuine in his voice. *Turns out love is black and white.* Estella involuntarily reached up and touched her hair. Only one person apart from Jasper and Horace knew it was really black and white.

It was all clear. Everything – her whole life – had come to that moment. Even Magda and Richard, horrible people though they were, had served a purpose, because indirectly they'd led her to Peter.

It was all right now. Her whole body eased.

Peter was still singing, his voice coming gently through the speakers.

I don't need the whole paint box
To paint a picture of you
Love's like words on a page
And they show you what's true...
Love in black and white

She tried to get rid of the stupid smile that stretched

across her face, but it was impossible. *Love*. That was the word. He loved her, and she him. *Love*. She had never known the word until then. Never said it. Never really understood it.

"I think he likes you," Chris said with a knowing waggle of his thick brows. "Two songs in the last few weeks. Must be a record! Come on, let's go do a little harmony."

Chris opened another door and motioned Estella through, then descended a set of steps leading into the main recording area – a blank open space with white walls and long mustard curtains. The floors were wood with carpets here and there. All over were space dividers cutting the room apart into a dozen nooks, each loaded with instruments, amplifiers, rolled foam and sandbags and coils of wires. In the middle of it all, alone on a high chair, facing one of the little cubicles against the wall, sat Peter and his guitar. He didn't hear them walk in, as he had on a set of green headphones. He was clearly deep in the song, strumming, feeling the music.

Chris began singing along, harmonising with Peter. Peter jumped and knocked off his headphones, almost dropping his guitar.

"Jumpy, jumpy," Chris said with a laugh. "Found Estella

outside, mate. Brought her in. You didn't leave her name up front."

Peter cocked his head, and a strange expression came over his face. He leaned around Chris to see where Estella stood.

"Stel?" he said. "I—"

"It's amazing," Estella cut in.

"What?"

"The song."

"Oh. Yeah..." He scratched his head for a moment. "Well, it's not quite right yet. Still got some kinks to work out."

"No," she insisted. "It's perfect."

Chris was looking at the wall, then back at Peter.

"Did you show Estella the control room?" Peter asked in an oddly formal voice. "She can hear so much better up there."

"Yessss..." Chris said, a note of hesitancy in his voice. "Yeah. Sure. The control room. Come on, Stel. That's really where the magic happens."

He put his arm over her shoulders and started to guide her back in that direction.

Estella threw a confused glance in Peter's direction that he didn't see – or pretended not to see. Something was off. Chris and Peter were trading looks. She stepped out from under Chris's arm and walked closer to Peter.

"Peter, what's going—" Estella's voice cut out as she looked towards the cubicle he'd been facing and realised there was someone else in the room. Peter had not been singing towards the wall – he had been singing at someone. To someone.

A girl.

20

HELLO, CRUEL HEART

THE GIRL in question was seated on a cushion, partly obscured by the cubicle, leaning with her back to the wall and her long legs stretched out in front of her. Estella had seen her somewhere in passing, maybe at the party they'd had the night the band was on the telly. Or somewhere else? That long black hair of hers was familiar.

"Oh," Peter said, feigning surprise, as though he'd just noticed the girl there himself. "Estella, this is Angie. Angie, do you know Estella?"

"I think we've met," the girl said with a small smile.

Angie Walker-Weatherford. The girl Estella had seen on the street that day with Magda's on-again, off-again boyfriend, the one Magda had so blithely disparaged.

Angie yawned and stretched her arms high, then lowered them, elbows out, with a smile. "Been *such* a long day," she said. "You know how it is with artists. I think I'll pop out for a cup of tea. Be back in a bit."

She peeled herself up from the floor ever so slowly, each limb unfolding as if in slow motion, and languidly made her way out of the room. Peter set down his guitar and started fussing with his headphones and wires.

"Peter. Can I talk to you?" Estella said.

He started, as though she hadn't just been standing in front of him. "Oh... sure. Come on."

Estella avoided looking at Chris as she followed Peter up the steps, through the control room and into the hall.

"There's a little kitchen down here, if you want a bite," Peter said, motioning for Estella to follow him.

"Peter," she said, gritting her teeth. "I don't care about the kitchen. Stop. I need to talk to you." But she was starting to forget why she had come in the first place. Her mind was fuzzy. "What is she *doing* here?" she heard herself asking.

"Angie?" he said. "She's... I was working out a song. I was playing it for her."

That much had been obvious.

"What are *you* doing here?" Peter asked.

"I went to your flat. You weren't home."

"You went to the flat? I didn't think... How did you know where... What for?"

"Because I—" Because she had nowhere to live. Because Magda and Richard had used and betrayed her. Because she had alienated the only true friends she'd ever had. "I needed to talk to you."

Peter didn't respond, suddenly seeming very interested in the clock on the wall. The clock got louder in Estella's ears. Or was that her heartbeat?

"Is she... Angie... with someone in the band?" she asked.

"I just needed someone to listen to the new song," he said again, evading the question.

What had Magda said about Angie? *Always wears white – seems to think it's her signature, which is hilarious.*

Black hair, white dress.

Love in black and white.

"You wrote her a song," Estella said slowly.

Peter shrugged, his cheeks colouring. "Well, yeah. That's

what I do. I write songs. About things, people... I'm in a band, Stel. I do it every day."

"But you wrote a song for *her*. 'Love in Black and White'."

"Look, Stel..." he said.

It was all he had to say. He reached out to try to touch her face. She stepped back.

"It doesn't change how I feel about you, honest it doesn't. No one is exclusive, right? You're my magic bean girl."

"No one is exclusive?"

More of Magda's words from Carnaby Street came back to her: *One mustn't be jealous or possessive.* But Estella had thought that was about other people, not something that applied to her and Peter. Because she and Peter had shared something. What about what Peter had said, that no one else was like the two of them?

Peter was still talking, but his words were falling apart in the air.

"It doesn't mean we can't still have our thing. Nothing has changed."

Except everything had changed. In that moment, every part of her broke open. The walls of the room seemed like they were rippling.

"What about the tour?" Estella asked. "About going to America?"

"What about it?" He looked genuinely confused.

"I'm supposed to go with you."

"I never said that," Peter replied.

"You asked... you asked if I wanted to see America."

"Sure," he replied, at least having the decency to look embarrassed. "But I was... I was just asking. I never... I'm sorry if you got the wrong idea. We can't take people on the tour. The record company, they don't let us. It's expensive, and..."

"But you said—"

"Excitement of the moment. I mean, sure, we could meet up in some places if you wanted to come, but..."

Estella had gone cold. Her body was stiff, numb.

Not even Cruella would come out for this.

The studio door opened and Chris peered out before approaching them cautiously.

"Hey," he said softly. "We need to get started soon. The others will be here, and we have our time scheduled to start in half an hour. Have to get set up."

"Coming," Peter said. He turned back to Estella once Chris had gone. "Look, I'll phone you later, okay?"

"Don't bother," she said. Of course, there was nowhere to phone. Not that she wanted him to. Still, she thought he'd protest, maybe even apologise, try to get her back. Instead he just shook his head as though he was disappointed in her.

"If that's what you want."

Estella turned her back. She waited to see if he would reach for her shoulder, turn her round, tell her it was all a mistake, he was sorry, they'd work it out right then, he loved her, she was his magic bean girl...

But she heard footsteps walking away. Another set walked towards her, and Chris was suddenly looming in front of her, leaning against the wall.

"Sorry, love," he said. "He's always doing this. Bit of a dark horse, our Peter. I guess all that song writing, he has to get the material from somewhere. I tried to tell you that first night."

You be careful with this one. He's trouble.

"I thought you were joking," she said, keeping her head down.

Chris looked at her, pity evident in his eyes. "I do think he really likes you, Stel. You've been around longer than most. You're likely better off without him. You've got a lot of talent. He might need you, but you don't need him, if I'm being honest."

He gave her shoulder a quick pat, then walked back down the hall. Estella heard the studio door close.

The moustachioed Mac peered at Estella over his desk as she walked through in a daze. Apparently he had overheard the entire exchange.

"These musician types," he said to her. "Not worth it, luv. I see it every day, sitting here. Every day."

She wanted to reply, but she couldn't form any words.

"You want to get yourself a nice young man from some other walk of life," he added. "Maybe a milkman, something like that. Leave these musicians be. No good comes of them, believe me. Every day. I see it every day. Bloody scoundrels, the lot of them."

The night Estella's mum died, there was rain.

Thunder, lightning. The real deal, a dark and stormy night. Estella remembered the sky cracking and splitting above the old mansion where that magnificent party had been held.

She'd thought that rainy night was the loneliest of her

life, but this one came a close second. As she walked through the streets, the rain beating down on her, soaking her clothes, her hair, her shoes, she felt nothing. That warm thing that had sparked in her, that flicker of love, had turned to ash. She went through all the rooms of her mind, and everywhere she found Peter, she smashed the place apart.

In the dark kitchen at the party – she tore the memory down.

Standing in the doorway of the attic at Magda and Richard's, that first day they really spoke. Smashed.

His long, tapered fingers making the ancient instruments sing. Gone.

The first kiss in the Lair; dancing until dawn at Stonehenge; running through the fields. All of it had to go.

Estella didn't cry. She hardened. She forced herself to grapple with the memory, experience it anew, let it wash over her and then she crushed it. And every time, she grew stronger.

From Peter, her mind's eye turned to Magda and Richard, who acquired and discarded people like they did all their possessions – clothes, houses, things. Estella had been useful for a time. Interesting and new, like a prized pet.

That was all she had ever been to them. An accessory.

How had she allowed it to happen? How hadn't she seen?

She didn't feel the wet, didn't step away when the cars splashed her with cold, dirty water. Let them. Let her take it all in, all the mess and the murk of cruel London. It couldn't break her.

I tried to tell you, Cruella said, surfacing for the second time that day. *None of this was for you. Love. Friendship. Those are weak ideas made up by weak people. Strong people – geniuses – they work alone. They believe in no one and nothing but themselves.*

Estella did not tell Cruella to go away. She didn't tell her to stop talking.

I take over from here. Just you and me. You could be something great, something those rich morons could never be. Trust me. I have never lied to you. I have always looked out for your best interests. See what happens when you ignore me?

"All right, Cruella," Estella said out loud. "You win."

Estella made her way to Regent's Park. She had the place to herself in the storm, so she sat on the edge of the familiar fountain and let the rain run over her eyes and down her skin. Maybe for one night she could find a shed in someone's yard while she plotted her next move. Or she could sleep under a bridge or in the shelter of one of those bombed-out walls at St Anne's Court.

Suddenly, Estella saw two people. One was short; one was tall. They carried lopsided and partially broken umbrellas. Estella thought she recognised the blurry shapes. She gave her eyes a hard rub, even though she knew that meant her already runny eye makeup would now be streaked all the way across her face.

Yes, one was Jasper. And beside him, Horace.

"As I thought," Jasper said, walking up to Estella.

At first, she was too astonished to know what to do. "How did you know I was here?" she finally asked.

"Well, you see," Jasper said, "word gets around. Someone said they thought you got nicked in Harrods."

"Sumfin about lime marmalade," Horace said, wrinkling his nose. "Disgusting choice. Have we taught you nothing?"

"So we made some enquiries around the nick up there. Someone said you'd been let out. So we went around to that fancy house of yours. We've been keeping an eye. We saw those people you live with packing up their things."

"I'm not going to be staying there any more," Estella said.

"Gathered that from the way that blonde bird was throwing your things out of the window," Horace said.

"So where were they off to? Didn't look like they were moving, but a lot of bags."

"They're going to Morocco," she said.

"What's that?" Horace asked.

"It's a country," she said. "In Africa."

"Sounds far."

"It is," she said.

"I take it you're not going," Jasper said.

"No."

Jasper nodded. "Figured. So we did the only reasonable thing," he continued. "We were curious. We're detectives now. They were being downright careless, leaving the door open while they were moving things around. Have to be careful. All sorts of people lurking about. So we went in. The girl was all upset because she said you'd been mean to her and now she couldn't find her address book, and you must have taken it. She's on the phone yelling to someone about it, saying she needed to find you and get it back, because all her important information's in there. We overhear something about a studio on St Anne's Court. So it's across town for us..."

"All over town," Horace said.

"And we get to this studio and who do we see but this fella you've been going around with, and he's..."

Here Jasper trailed off.

"With another girl," Estella finished for him. She noted that her nose was running, and she wiped it with the back of her hand. Was she crying? She couldn't tell, being out in the storm.

"With another girl," Jasper echoed, his voice a bit softer.

"Not pretty," Horace added.

"Followed them a bit, heard them saying how you'd left. That you'd surprised them. A guy joined them, gave them both an earful, saying your fella should have treated you better. At this point, we start to get a picture. You're not staying at that fancy house, and this bloke has done a dirty deed." Jasper spread his hands apart. "Once we saw that, we came here."

"Why here?"

"It's where you always go when something's wrong," he said.

She'd never thought about it, but it was true. Estella simply knew to come to this spot, the one that had represented so much hope when she and her mum had started off on their ill-fated trip to London. The place where she'd met Jasper and Horace for the first time.

"They used me," she said, bitterness edging her voice. "To make their stupid clothes. All of them. They used me."

"Tried to tell you that," Horace pointed out.

Estella kept her head down.

"I'm sorry," she finally said.

There was a long moment of silence.

"These things happen," Jasper finally said. "It wasn't you, anyway. It was Cruella."

"But I am Cruella. Cruella is me."

"Not to us. Doesn't matter anyway."

She listened to the raindrops landing on the surface of the water in the fountain. It was a soft sound, soothing. The rain had slowed somewhat, turning into something almost gentle, cleansing.

"You want to come home?" Jasper asked.

Estella turned to look at him, her mouth hanging open. How could they want her back after everything she'd put them through? After acting the way she had?

Because they're your family.

Cruella was beginning to make more and more sense.

"Come on," he said. "It was a row. Wink and Buddy keep pacing around. Do you want to?"

"Yeah," Estella replied. "I want to come home."

Jasper stood and offered her a hand up. It would be a bit much to take it, even though she was moved by the gesture. She pushed herself up and she pushed her feelings down. Jasper and Horace were fine, but no one else from then on. No Magdas and Richards taking advantage. And certainly, absolutely no Peters. No one ripping her to shreds. Ever again.

Horace and Jasper made room for her under their busted umbrellas, and the trio began walking out of the park.

"Some good news, though," Horace said. "Got that car I wanted."

"You did?"

Horace held up a set of keys.

"Turns out he can drive," Jasper said, sounding more than a little impressed.

"I learned from telly, and I read a book about it. Nothing to it."

"Where did you get a car?"

That was when Estella noticed the Electric Teacup's VW

van parked at the kerb. Well, not parked, precisely. It was jammed into a space on a diagonal, barely a hair's width away from a postbox.

"They were all so busy talking," Jasper explained. "We simply relieved them of their keys. Give it a nice paint job, get a new number plate... we'll have it good as new in no time."

He slid open the door, revealing all of Peter's instruments still inside.

"Nice guitars," Jasper said with a grin. "Really want to work on my playing. Think I might have a future as a musician. Keyboard in here, as well. Nice kit."

Estella climbed in with her friends, resisting the urge to laugh. They were safe out of the rain, together again.

"It's a good thing you got this van," she said. "We'll need it for all the stuff we're going to be carrying."

"Stuff?" Jasper said, turning around in the passenger's seat.

"They're off to the airport by now," she said with a smile. "Magda and Richard. We're going to rob their house, right down to the nails in the walls. And when we're done with them..."

She held up Magda's gold address book, dampened from the day's rain but overall no worse for wear. Jasper grinned back at her.

Horace started the engine and moved through the gears, and they drove off into the rainy London night.

ACKNOWLEDGEMENTS

THANK YOU to my editor, Elana Cohen, who made this happen, even while a global pandemic was going on. And as always, to my agent, Kate Schafer Testerman.